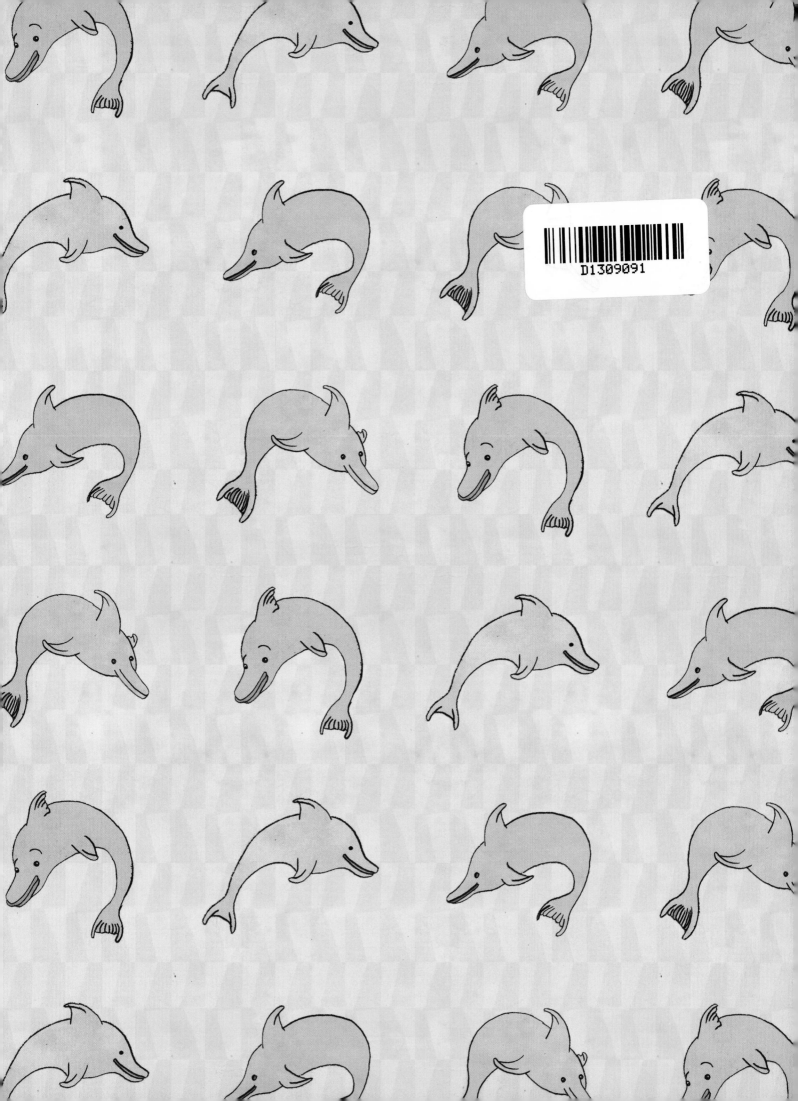

For Aya, Aya, Michal, and Noa, from Rutu

First published as *Ambatyam*
by Am Oved, Tel Aviv, 2001

First Restless Books hardcover edition October 2019

Hardcover ISBN: 9781632062116
Library of Congress Control Number: 2018948278

Cover design by Jonathan Yamakami
Cover illustration by Rutu Modan

This book is made possible by the New York State Council on the Arts
with the support of Governor Andrew M. Cuomo and the New York State Legislature.
This project is supported in part by an award from the National Endowment for the Arts.

NATIONAL ENDOWMENT for the ARTS arts.gov

NEW YORK STATE OF OPPORTUNITY. Council on the Arts

Printed in China

1 3 5 7 9 10 8 6 4 2

Restless Books, Inc.
232 3rd Street, Suite A101
Brooklyn, NY 11215

restlessbooks.org
publisher@restlessbooks.org

The Mermaid in the Bathtub

by Nurit Zarchi

Illustrations by Rutu Modan

Translated from the Hebrew by Tal Goldfajn

YONDER
Restless Books
for Young Readers

The day Mr. Whatwillltheysay found a mermaid sitting in his best armchair, he ran out of his apartment and wandered the streets until evening.

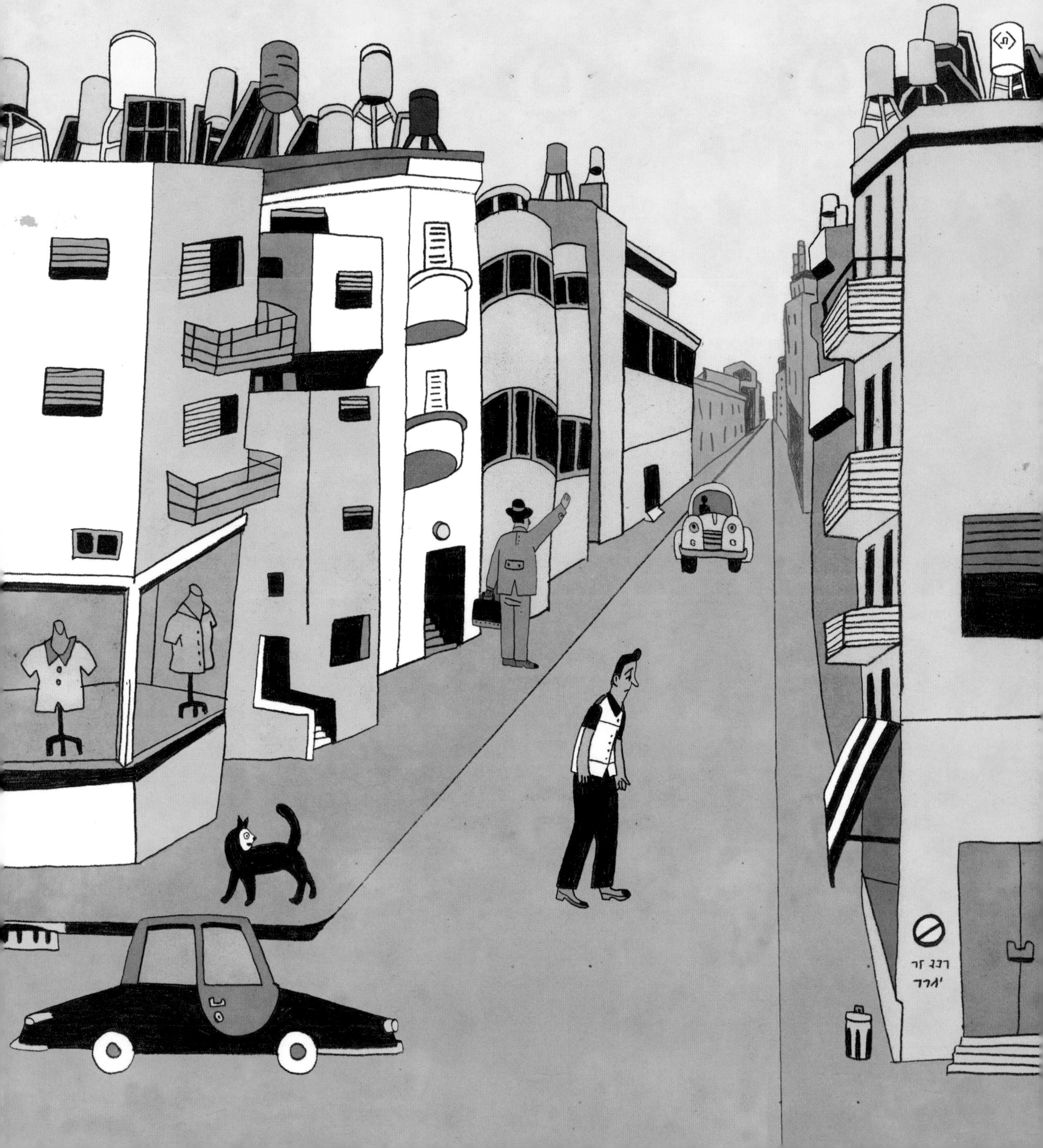

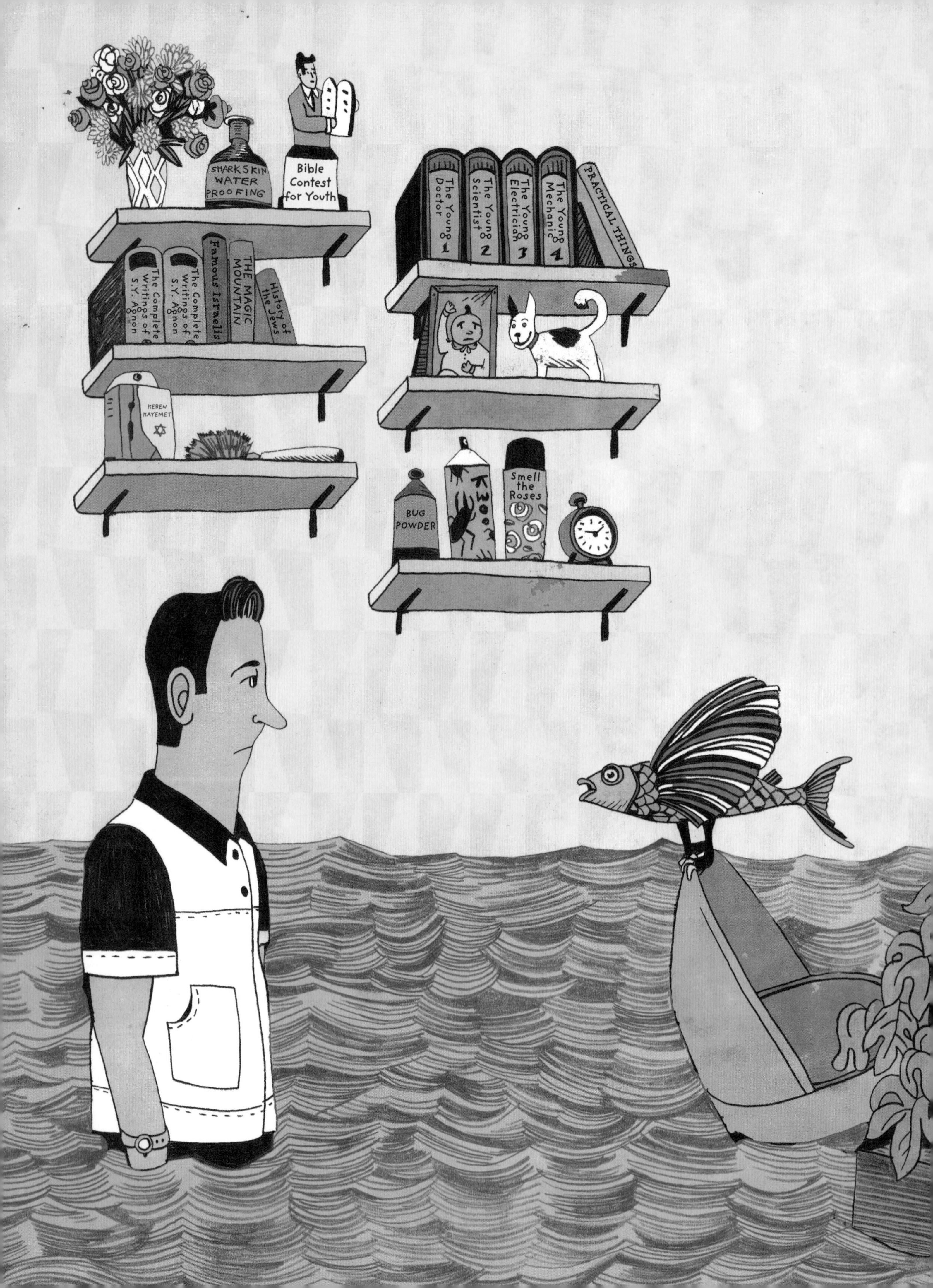

SHARKSKIN WATER PROOFING
Bible Contest for Youth
The Complete Writings of S.Y. Agnon
The Complete Writings of S.Y. Agnon
Famous Israelis
THE MAGIC MOUNTAIN
History of the Jews
The Young Doctor 1
The Young Scientist 2
The Young Electrician 3
The Young Mechanic 4
PRACTICAL THINGS
KEREN KAYEMET
BUG POWDER
K300
Smell the Roses

When he came back home, he saw that she was still sitting there in the armchair, which was now floating in the middle of the living room.

He looked at her and said: "Half of you is really lovely, but I could never, ever get married to a fish. Just imagine what they would all say."

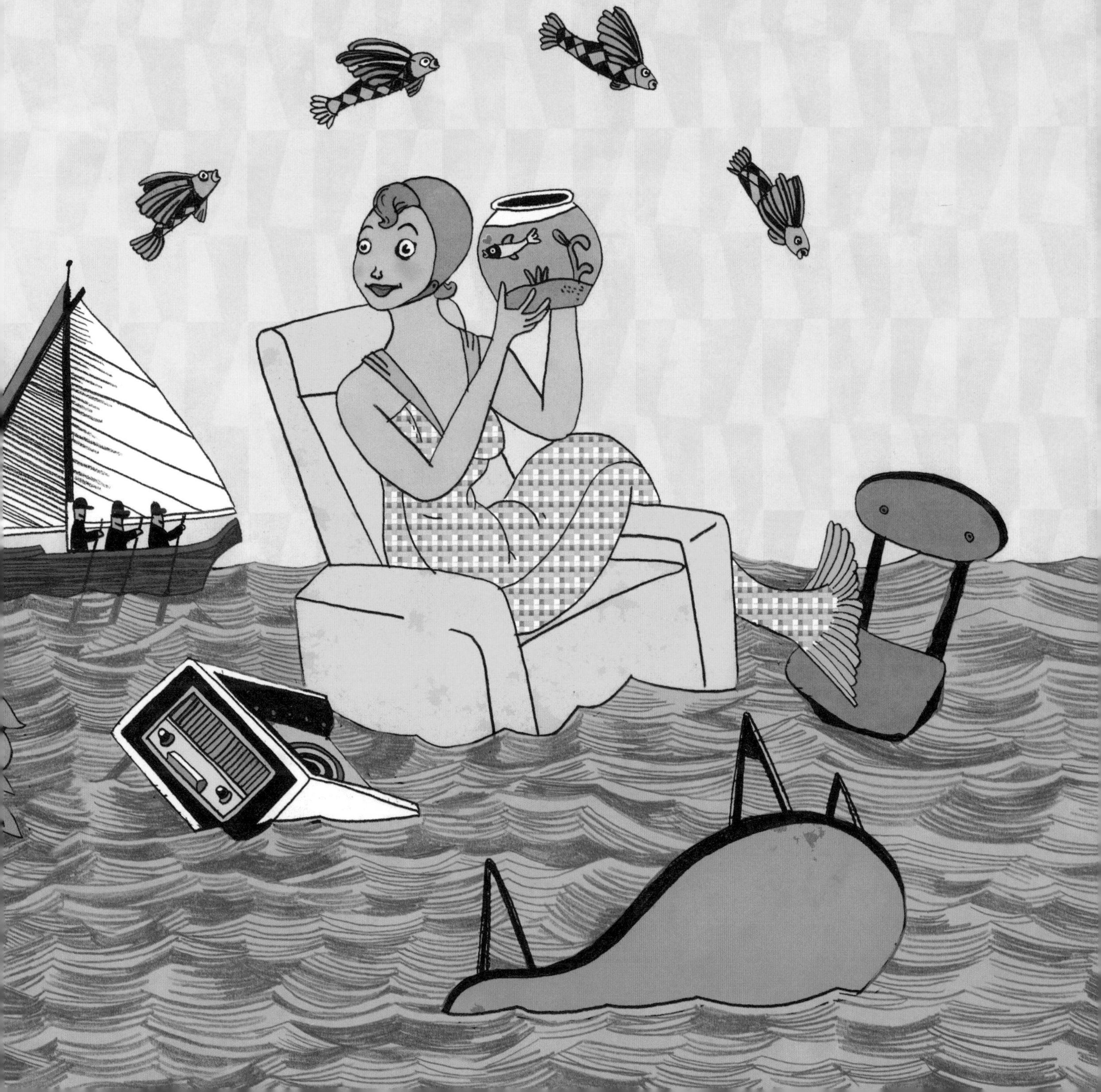

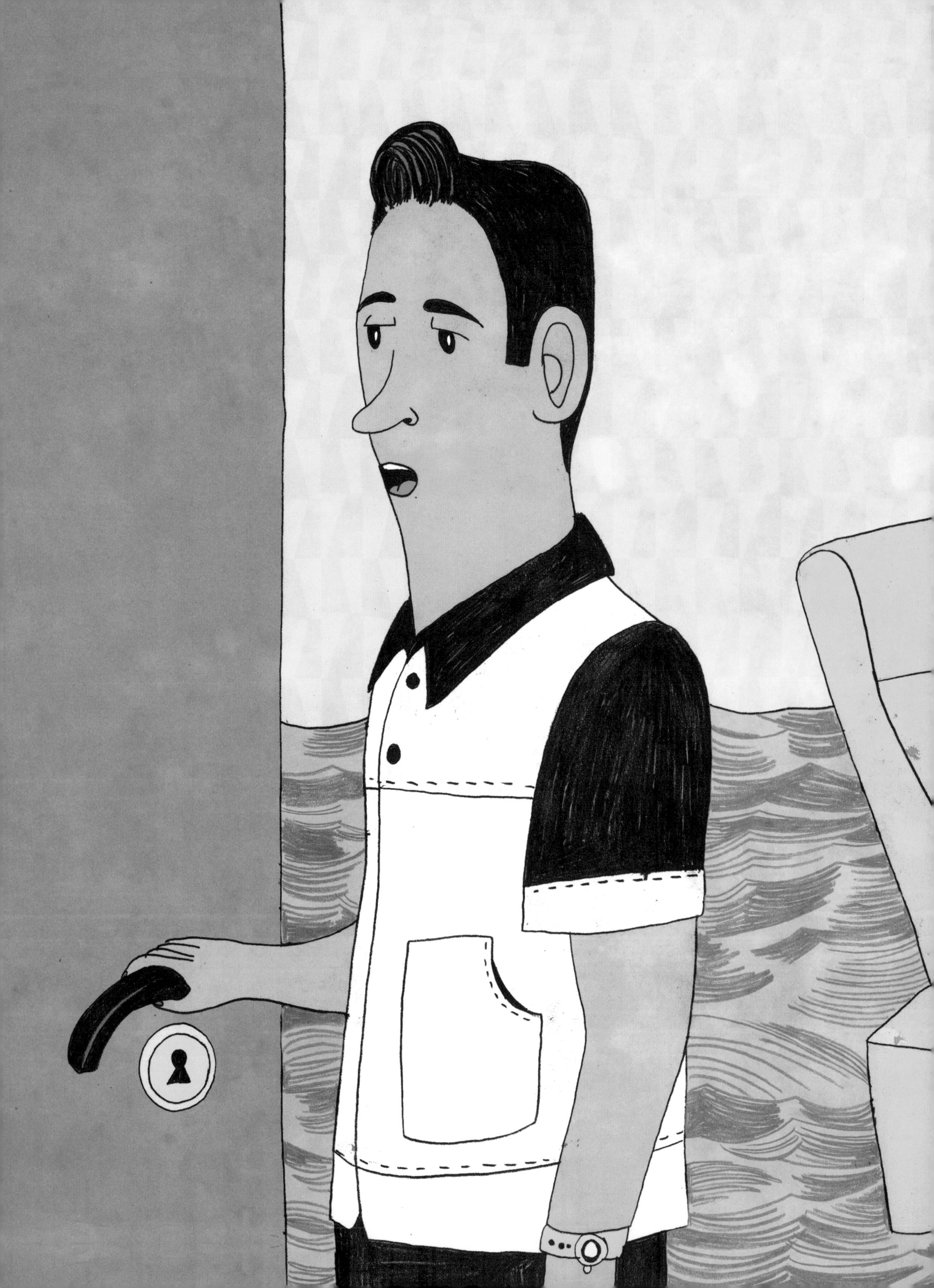

"You're saying that because you have legs," replied Grain-of-Sand. "If you don't want me, I can leave."

"Not right now," said Mr. Whatwilltheysay. "Not when everyone can see you. You can stay in the bathtub until nighttime."

And he left again to wander the streets until his apartment emptied.

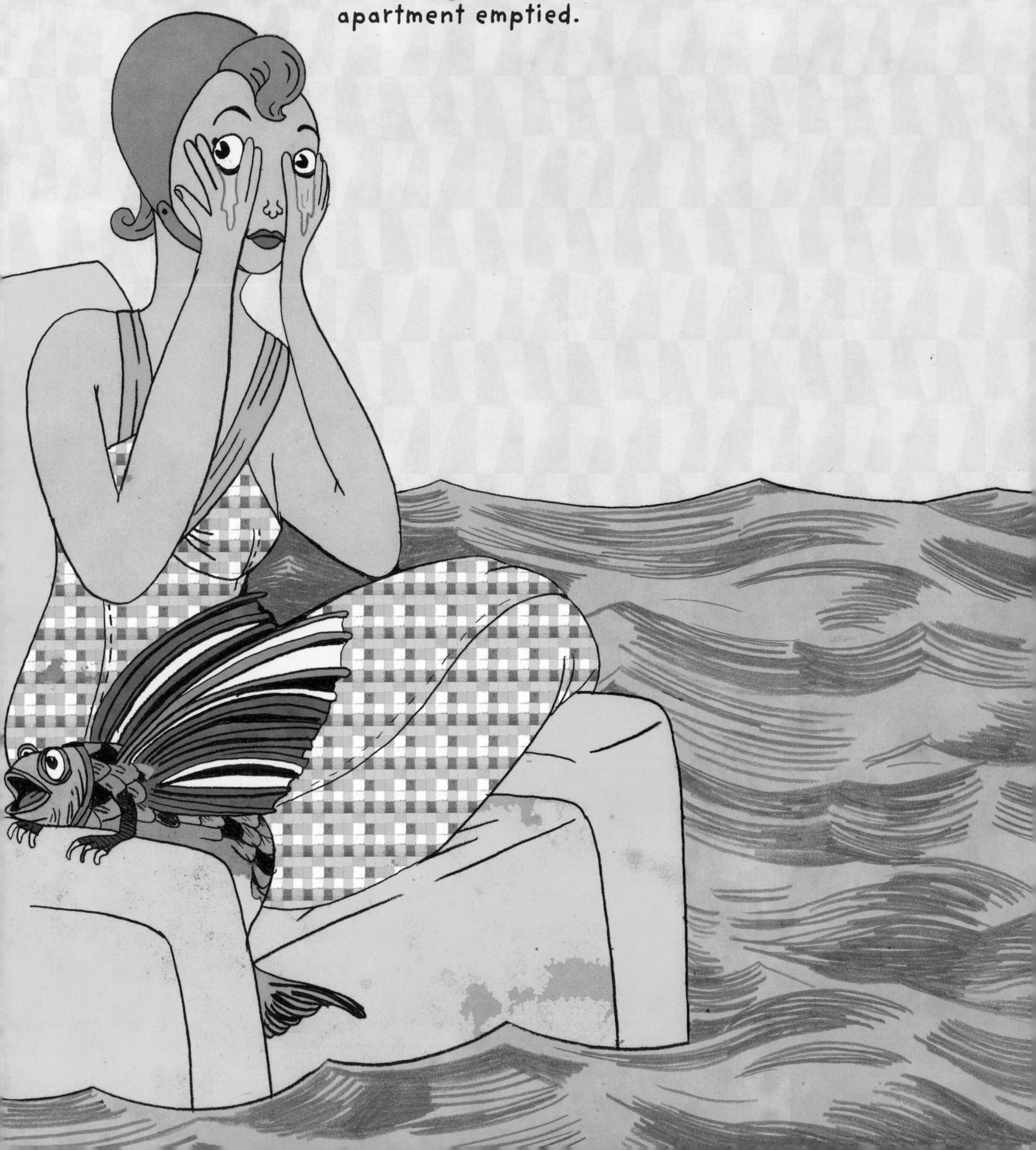

When he returned from his wandering, the door handle was dripping with water, as were the floor, the bedsheets, and the pillows. Mr. Whatwilltheysay tried to turn on the lights, but they wouldn't work.

"I wanted to leave," said Grain-of-Sand, "but I couldn't pack my things in the dark."

"Fine, then, but you have to leave first thing tomorrow."

Now the chairs, the dining table, and the newspapers were floating in the room.

"What are you doing?" asked Mr. Whatwilltheysay.

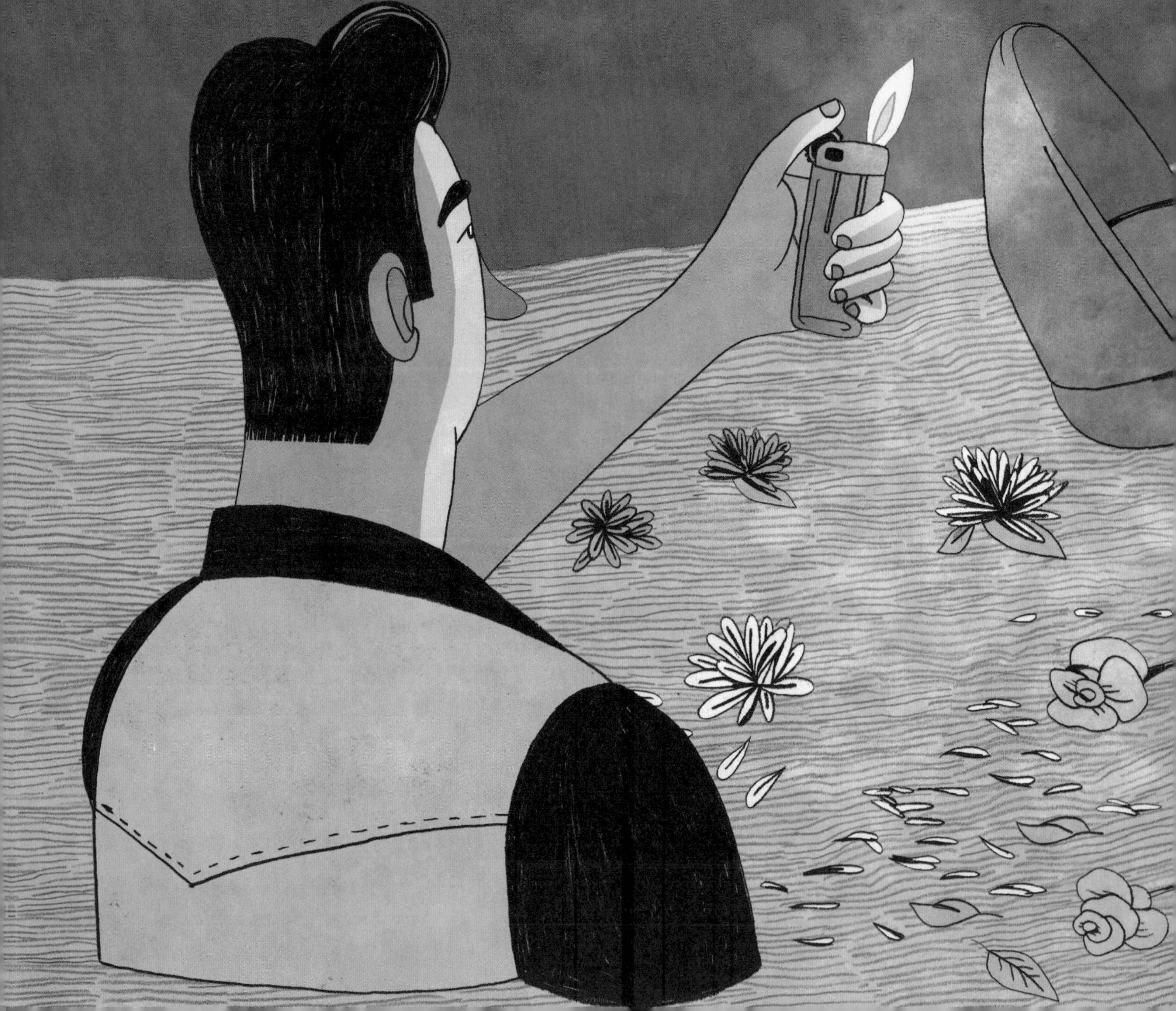

"Everything flows," replied Grain-of-Sand. "There's no point in pretending it isn't so."

"But the water will flood into the neighbors' apartments."

"That will be good for them," said Grain-of-Sand.

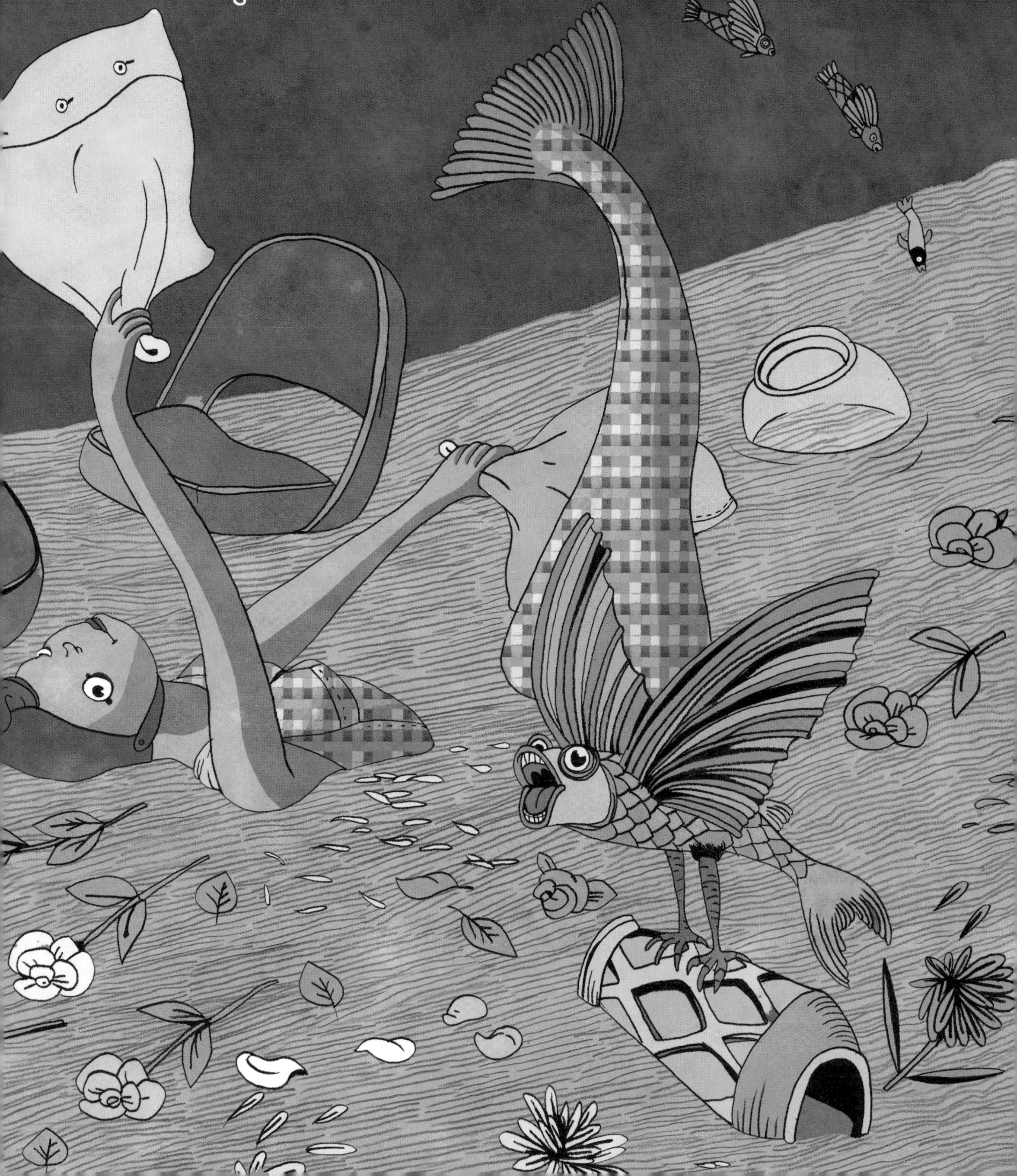

That night, Grain-of-Sand remained afloat in the sink
and sang songs of ships and lost treasures...

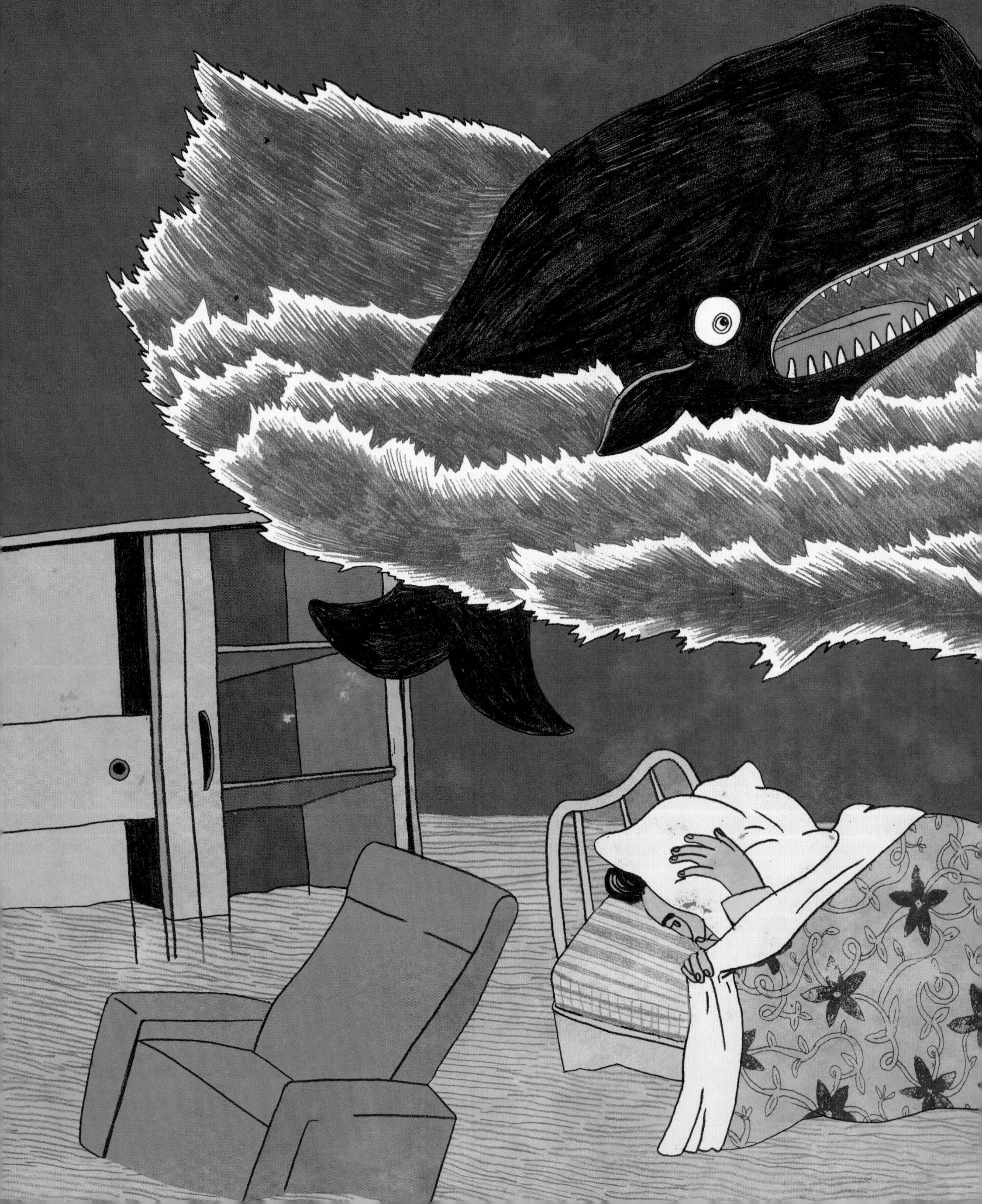

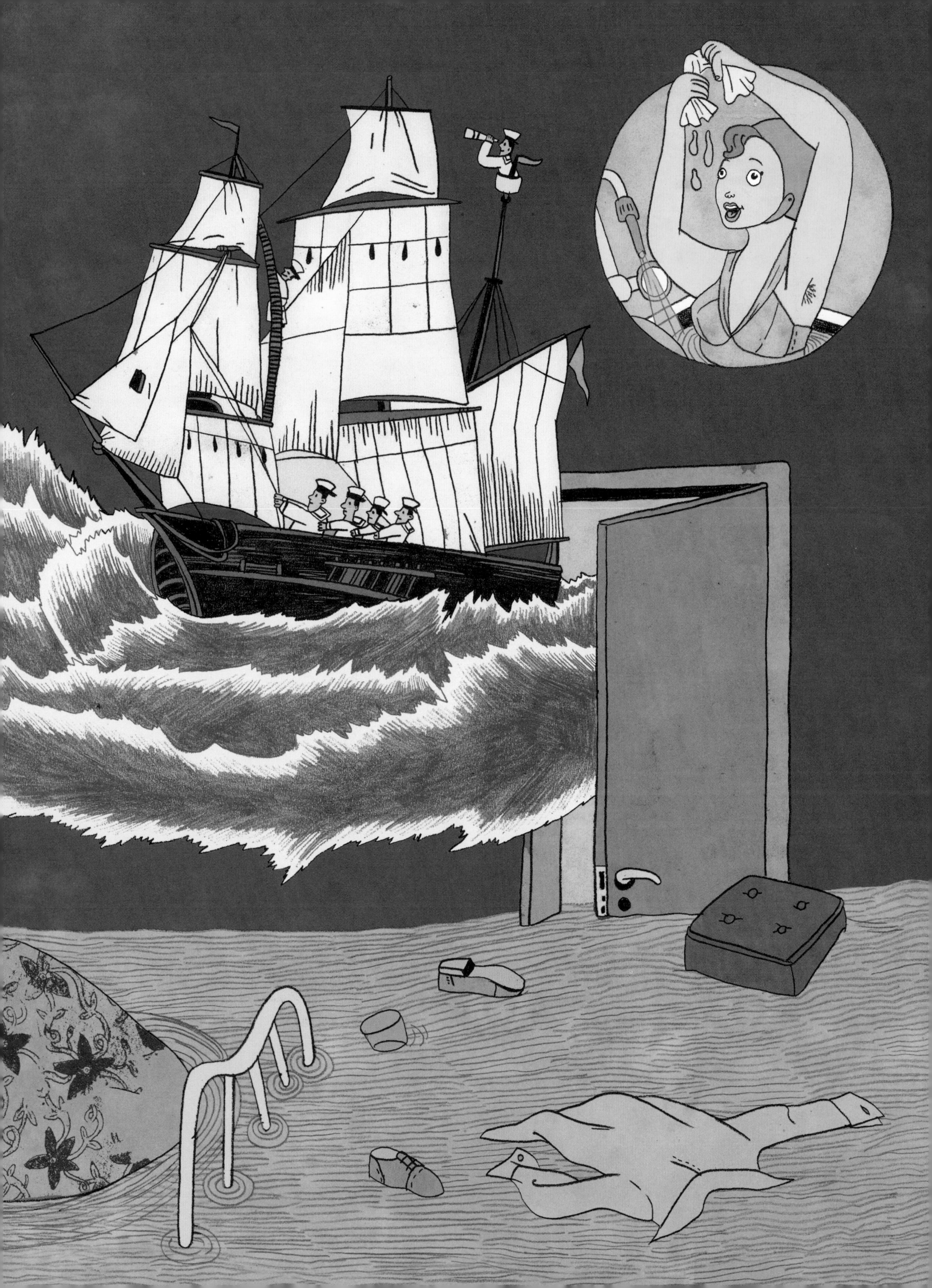

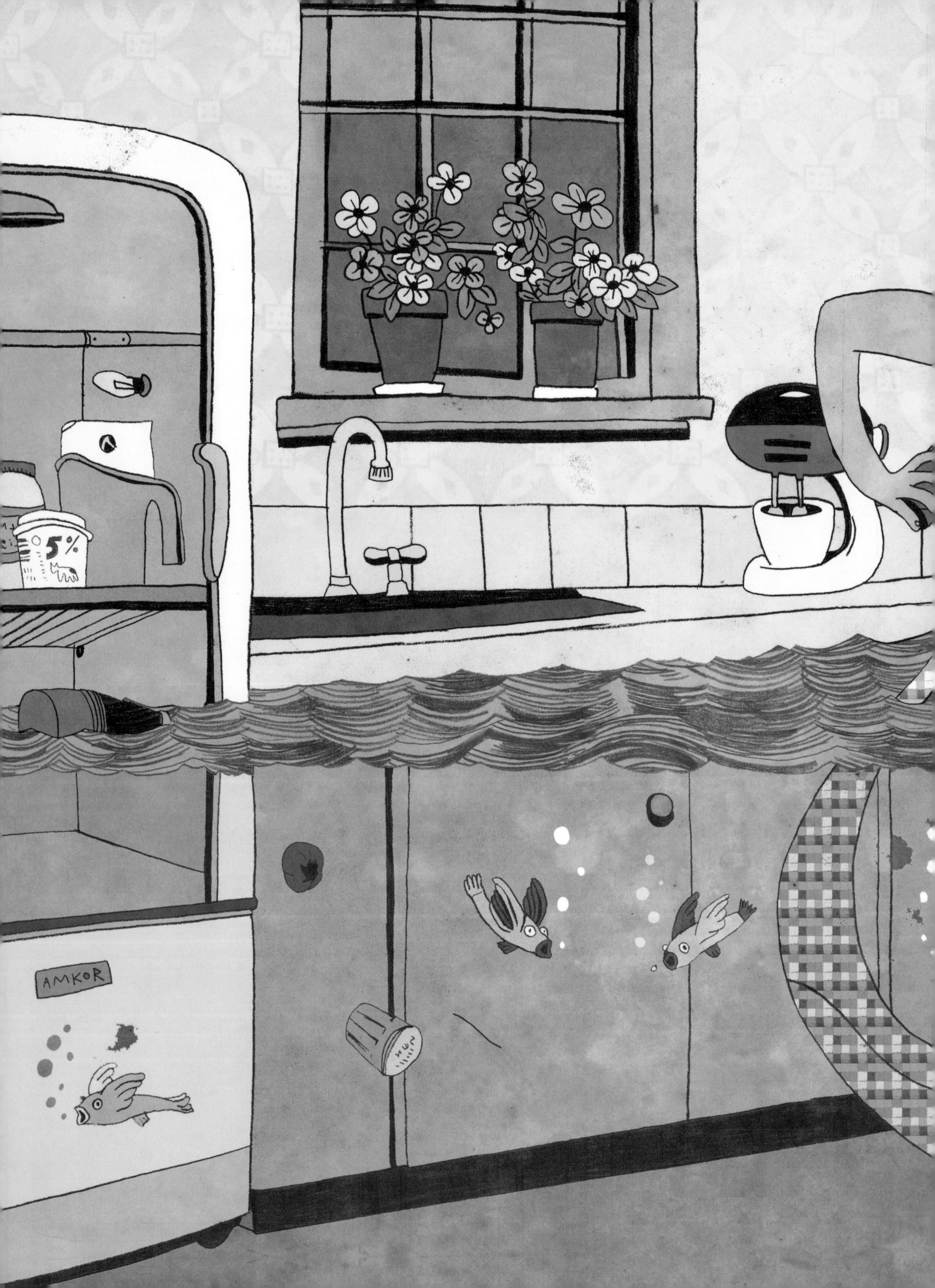
5%
AMKOR

On the second day, Mr. Whatwilltheysay woke up to the sound of Grain-of-Sand singing. "How strange that a fish can sing," he said.

"Everything sings," said Grain-of-Sand. "But this is my farewell song. If nobody wants me, if nobody wants to be my friend, I will leave."

"Don't be offended," said Mr. Whatwilltheysay, and looked at Grain-of-Sand's curly blue hair. "It's just that I can't stand it when everything is so slippery! It's dangerous, and someone could fall."

"You must learn to be careful," said Grain-of-Sand, "but if you don't want to practice, I can go."

"Now, when everyone can see you? You can't go outside without the proper clothing."

But Mr. Whatwilltheysay didn't have any clothes that would fit her. He left the house, while Grain-of-Sand remained.

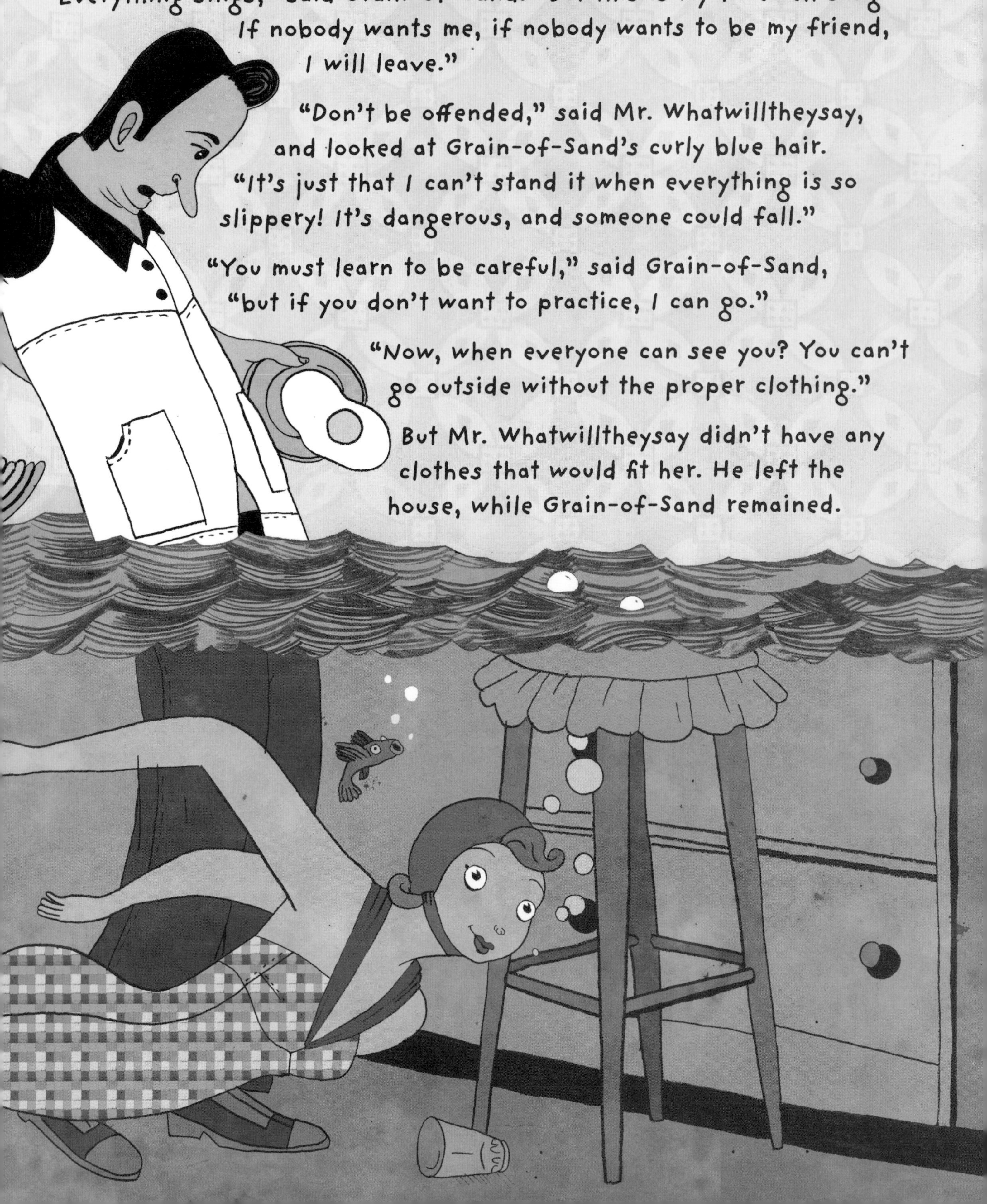

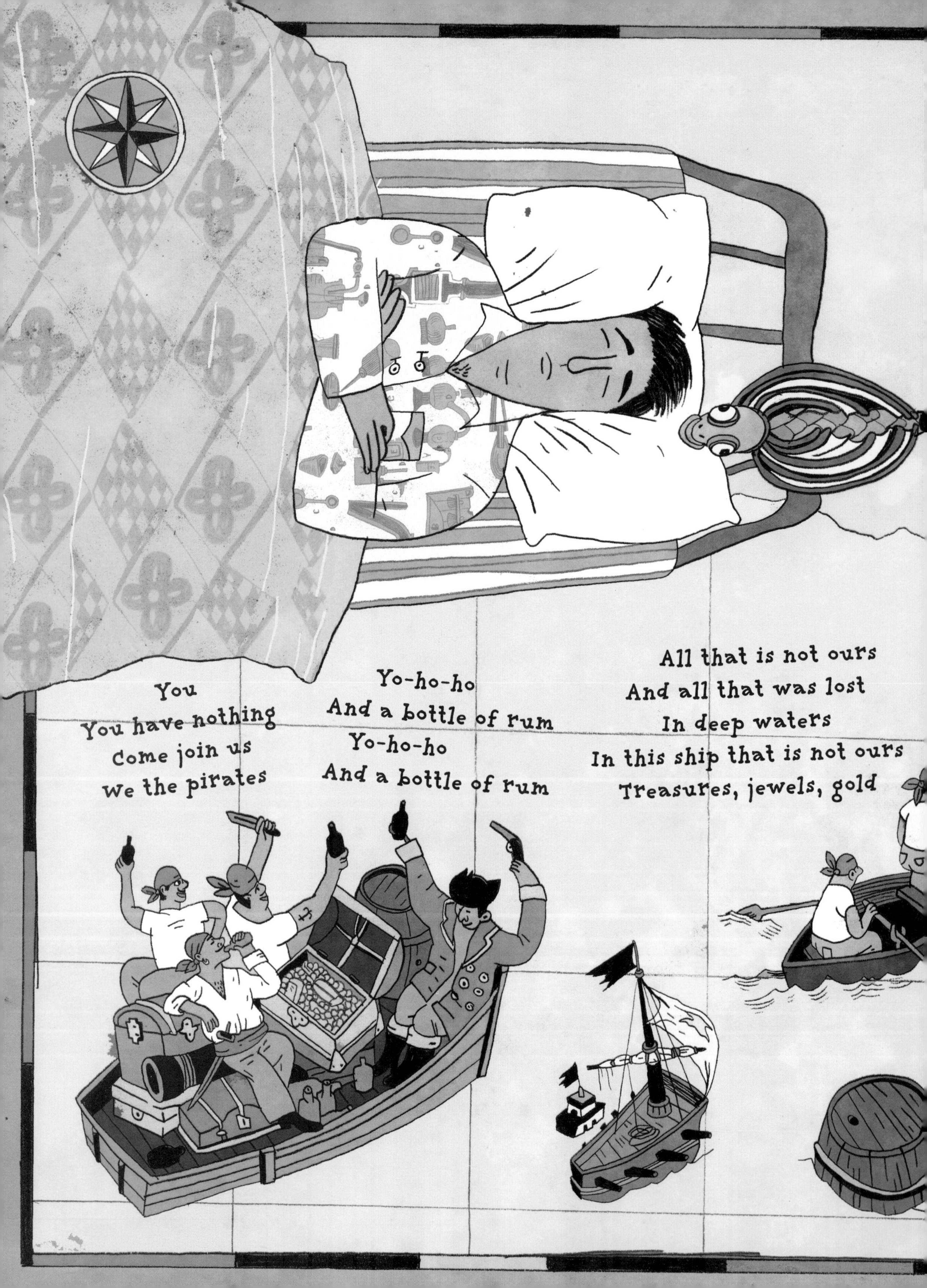

You
You have nothing
Come join us
We the pirates

Yo-ho-ho
And a bottle of rum
Yo-ho-ho
And a bottle of rum

All that is not ours
And all that was lost
In deep waters
In this ship that is not ours
Treasures, jewels, gold

When Mr. Whatwilltheysay returned home that evening, he was coughing and sneezing, and he gobbled two aspirins before going to bed. That night Grain-of-Sand sang him songs of pirates and ghost ships.

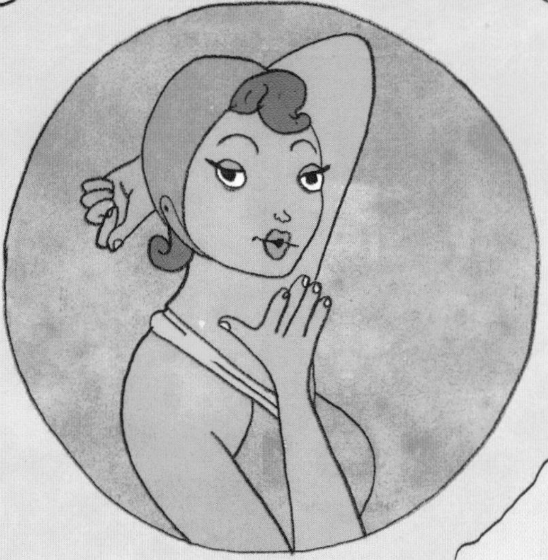

The waves are high
The mast is crooked
The heart is slant
The horizon,
Blurred
You, you,
Come join us

A few tempests
More
And we'll
Take it all

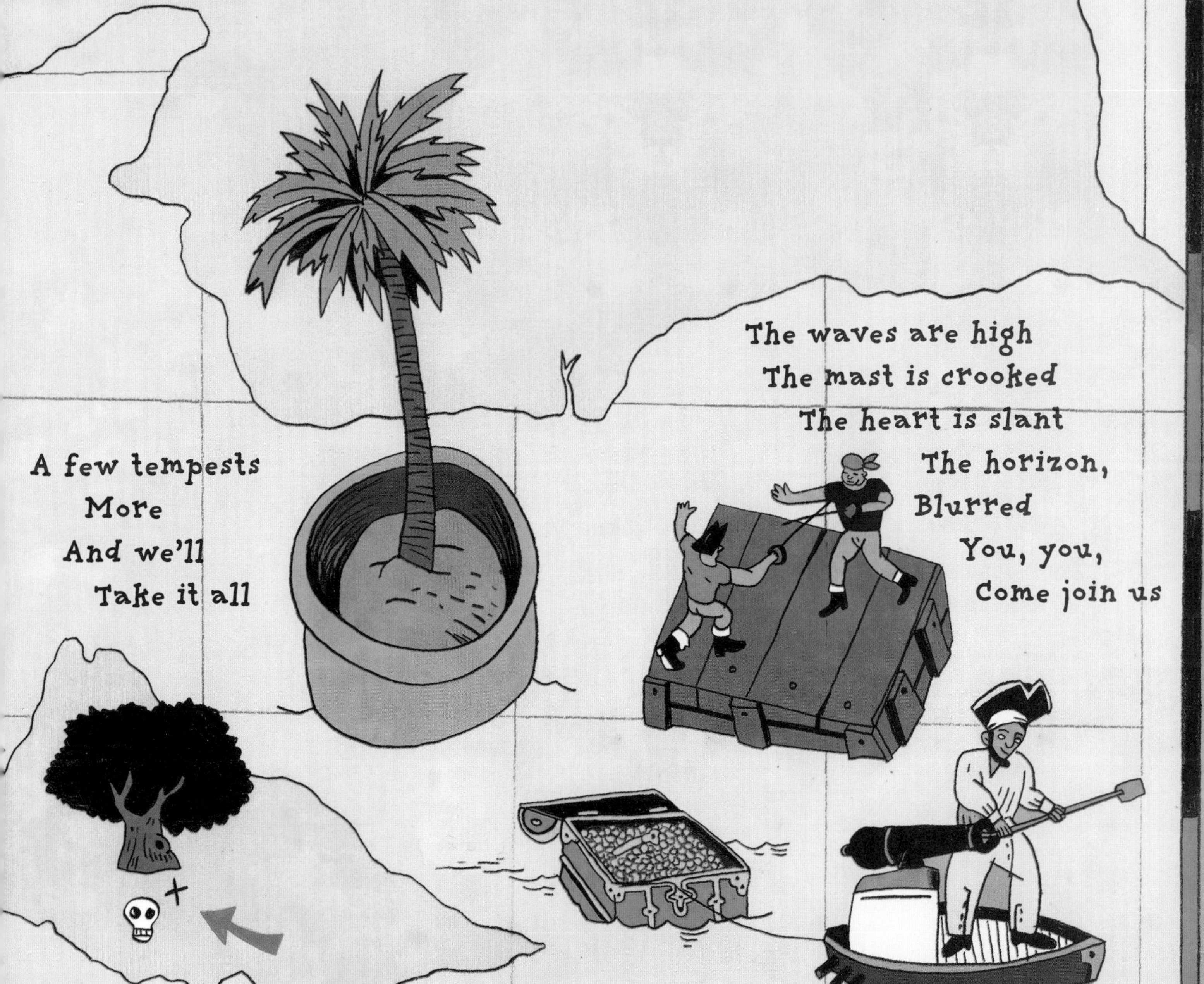

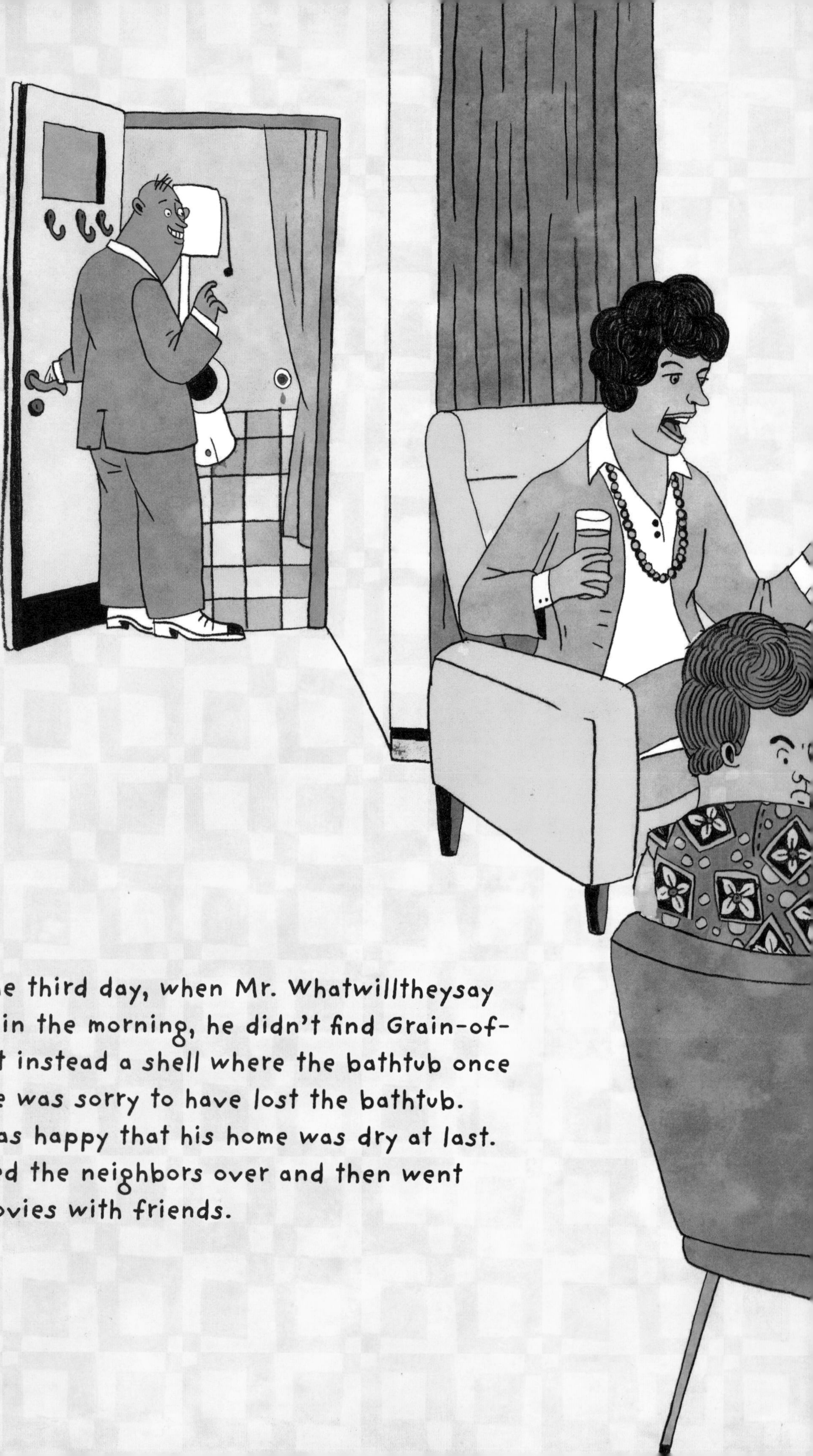

But on the third day, when Mr. Whatwilltheysay woke up in the morning, he didn't find Grain-of-Sand, but instead a shell where the bathtub once stood. He was sorry to have lost the bathtub. But he was happy that his home was dry at last. He invited the neighbors over and then went to the movies with friends.

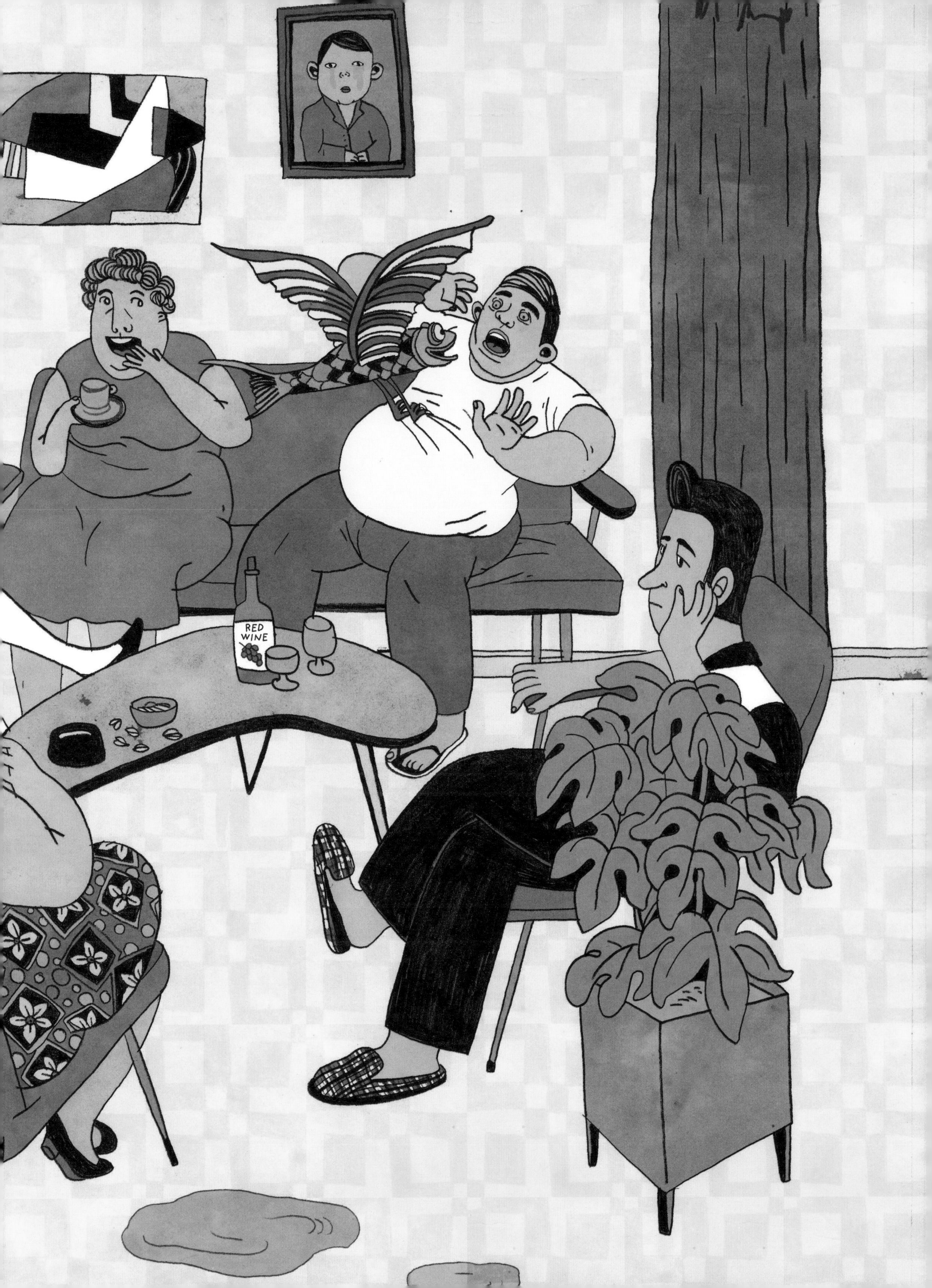
RED
WINE

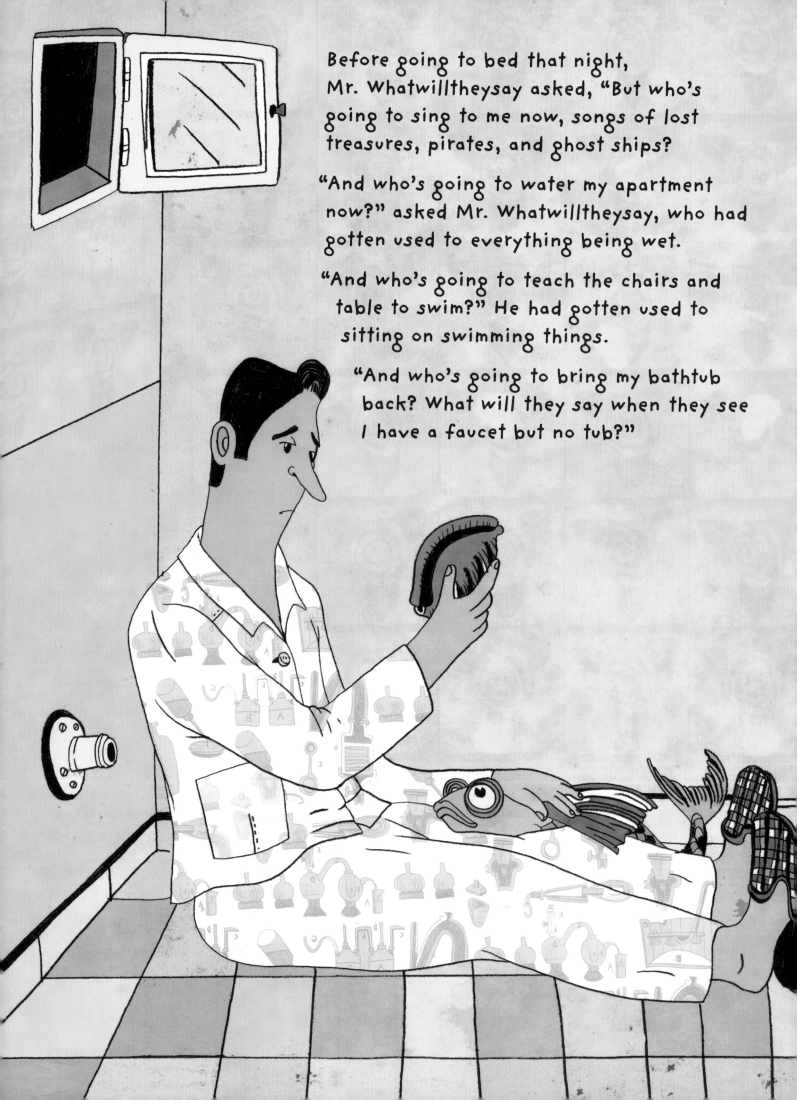

Before going to bed that night, Mr. Whatwilltheysay asked, "But who's going to sing to me now, songs of lost treasures, pirates, and ghost ships?

"And who's going to water my apartment now?" asked Mr. Whatwilltheysay, who had gotten used to everything being wet.

"And who's going to teach the chairs and table to swim?" He had gotten used to sitting on swimming things.

"And who's going to bring my bathtub back? What will they say when they see I have a faucet but no tub?"

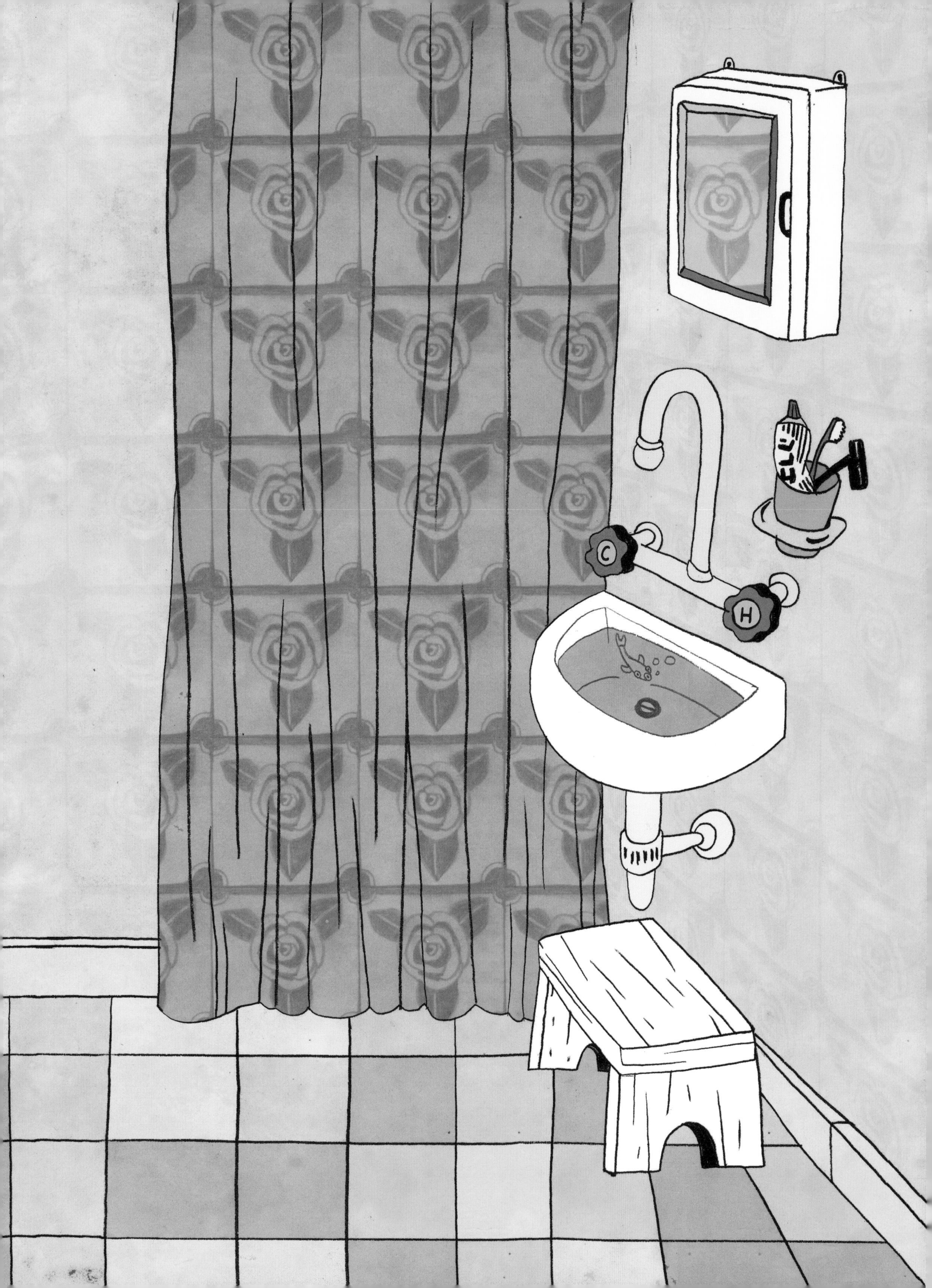
C
H

When the rain came, Mr. Whatwilltheysay thought: "It's all wet anyway." He took his umbrella and went out to look for Grain-of-Sand.

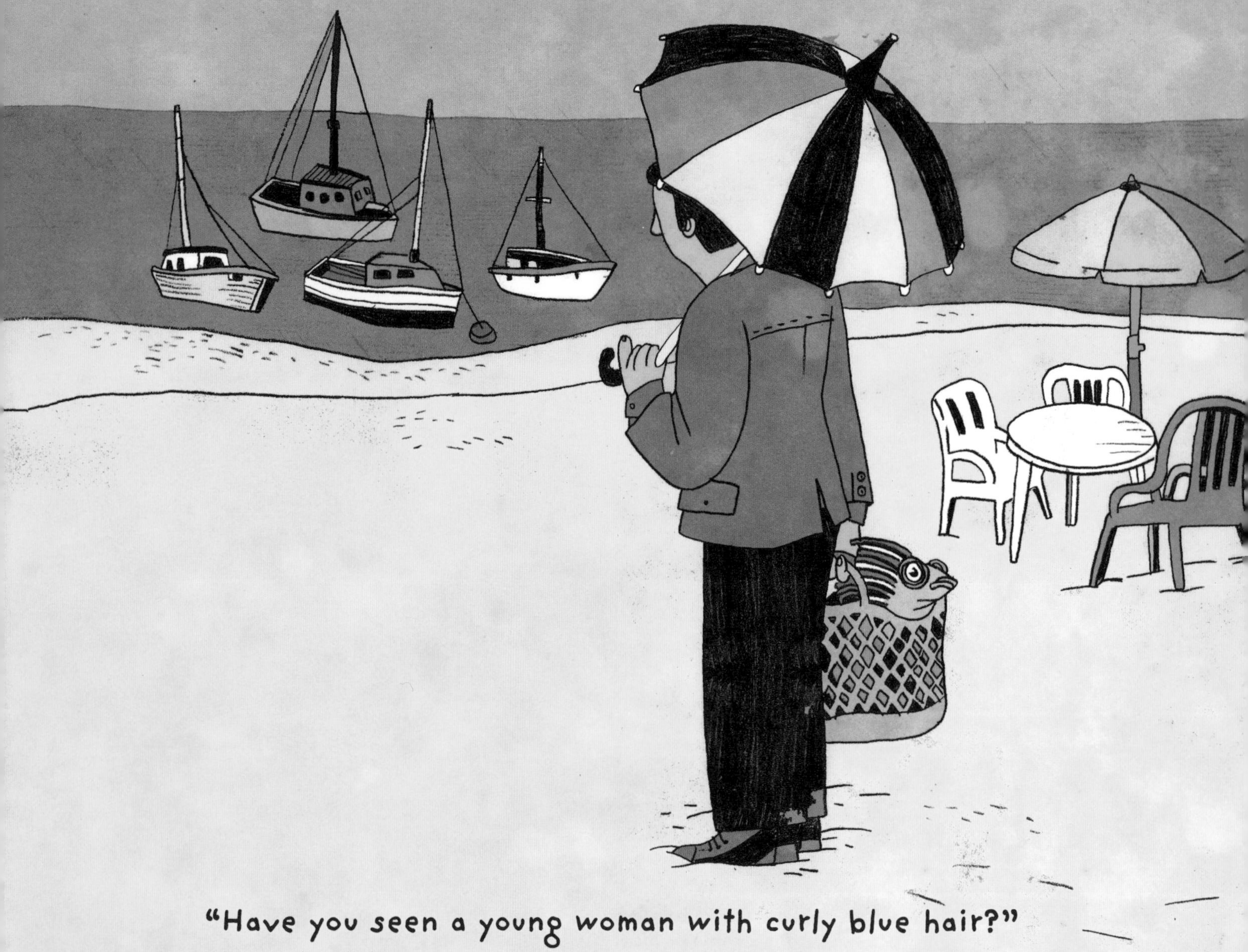

"Have you seen a young woman with curly blue hair?" he asked the passersby.

"Who knows how girls color their hair these days," they answered.

"Have you seen a young woman in a bathtub passing by?" he asked at a seaside café.

"There are all kinds of boats these days," answered the people in the café, and looked at him in a funny way.

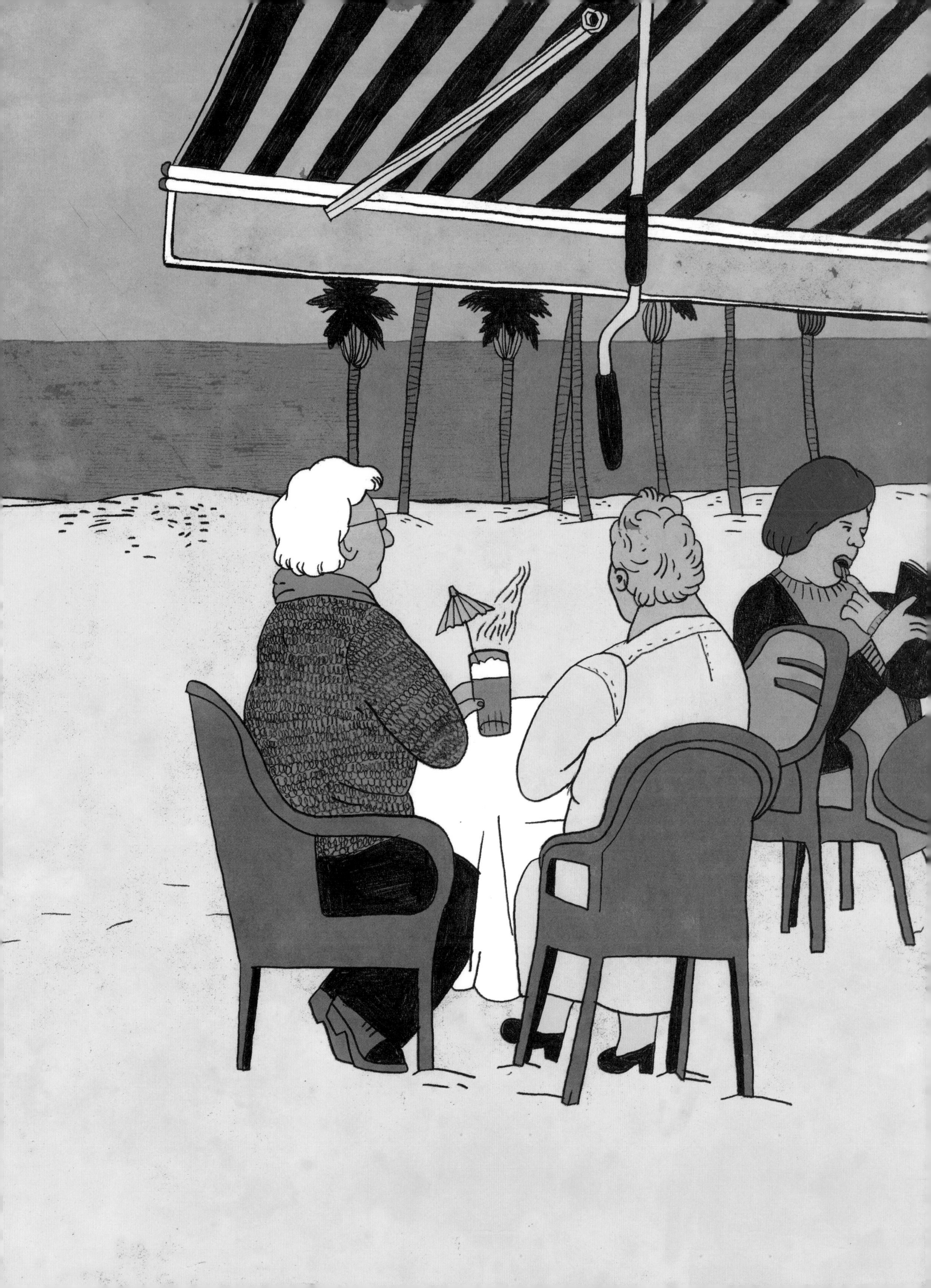

"Have you seen a young woman with a tail of a fish?" Mr. Whatwilltheysay asked the fishermen who were fixing their nets on the shore.

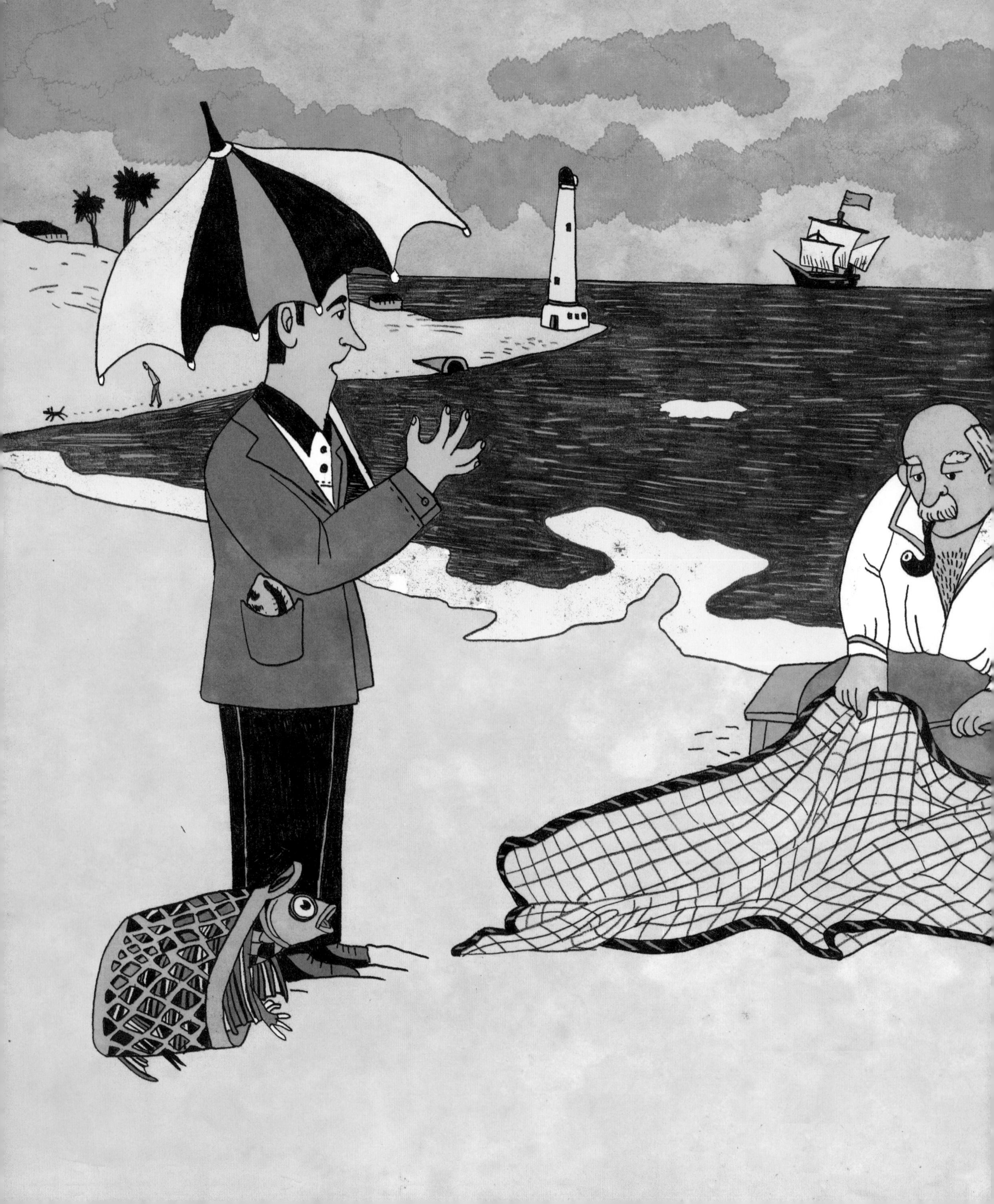

"You should really look for that sort of thing at night," said the fishermen, "when the big fish come out." They went back to fixing their nets.

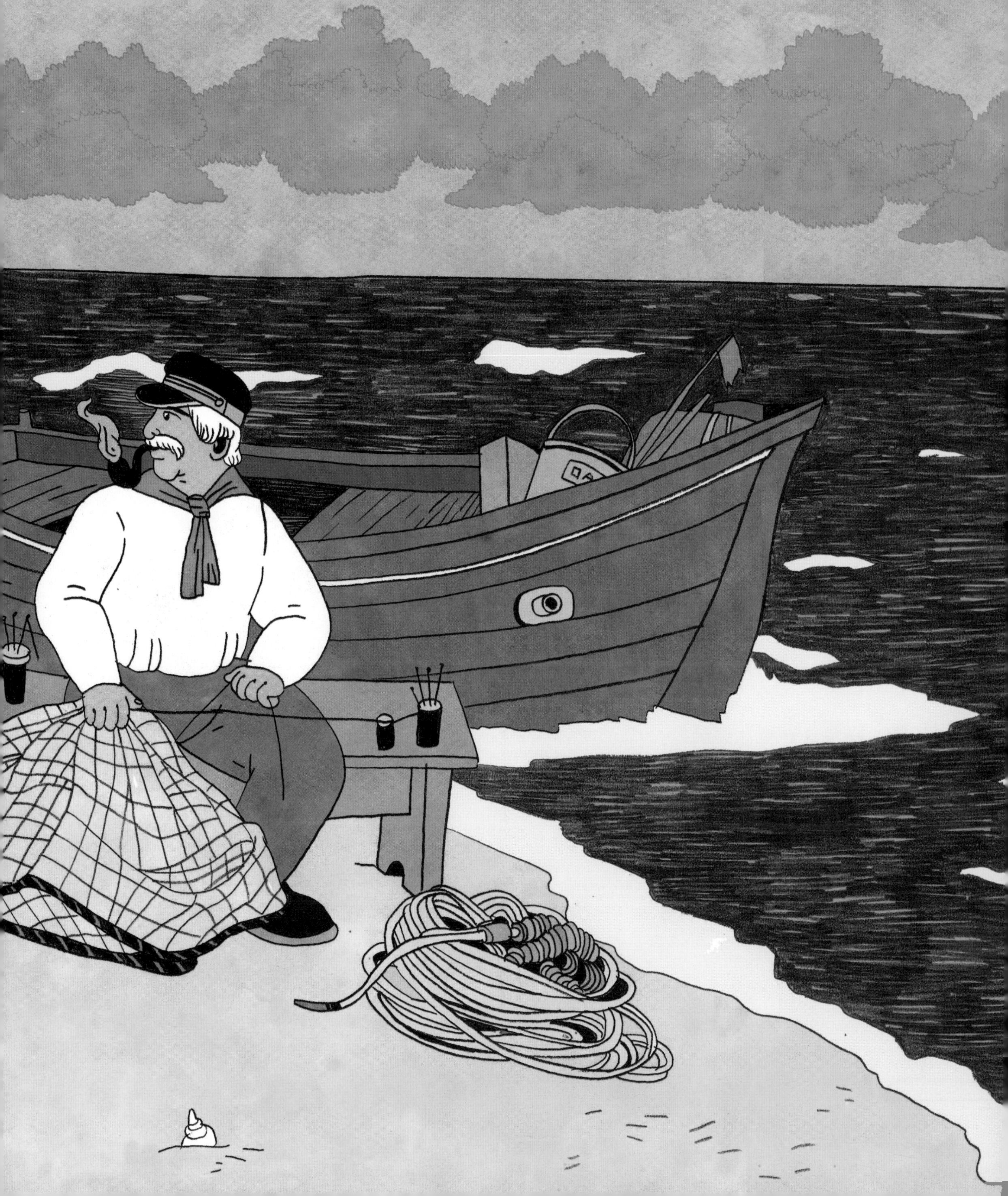

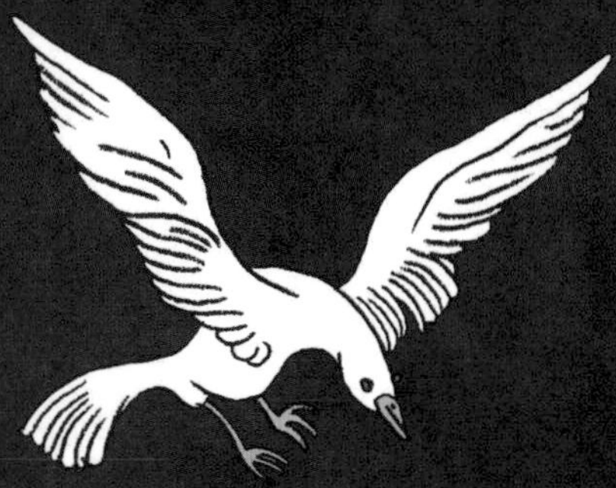

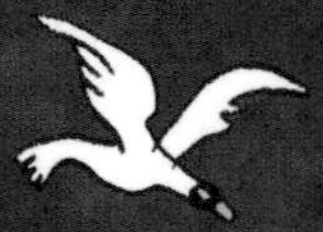

For three nights Mr. Whatwilltheysay waited on the shore until, on the fourth night, a yellow pancake moon rose over the sea.

Mr. Whatwilltheysay stood on the bow of a fishing boat and sang:

> Grain-of-Sand, Grain-of-Sand
> Come back to me
> From the dark blue.
> Come back to me, blue curl,
> In spite of it all.

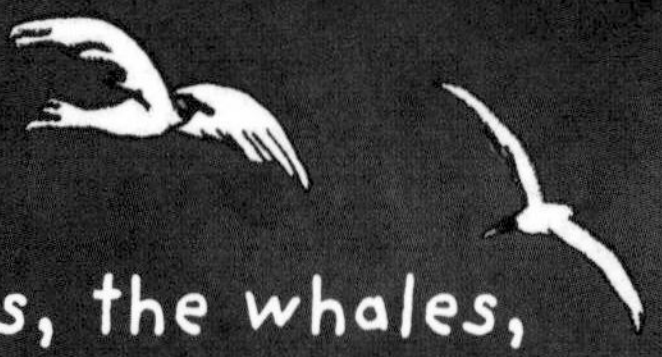

The sea glowed and glimmered silver.

From the darkness, the voices of the waves, the whales, the dolphins, and the moon birds replied, echoing his song:

> Grain-of-Sand, Grain-of-Sand
> Come back to him,
> In spite of it all.

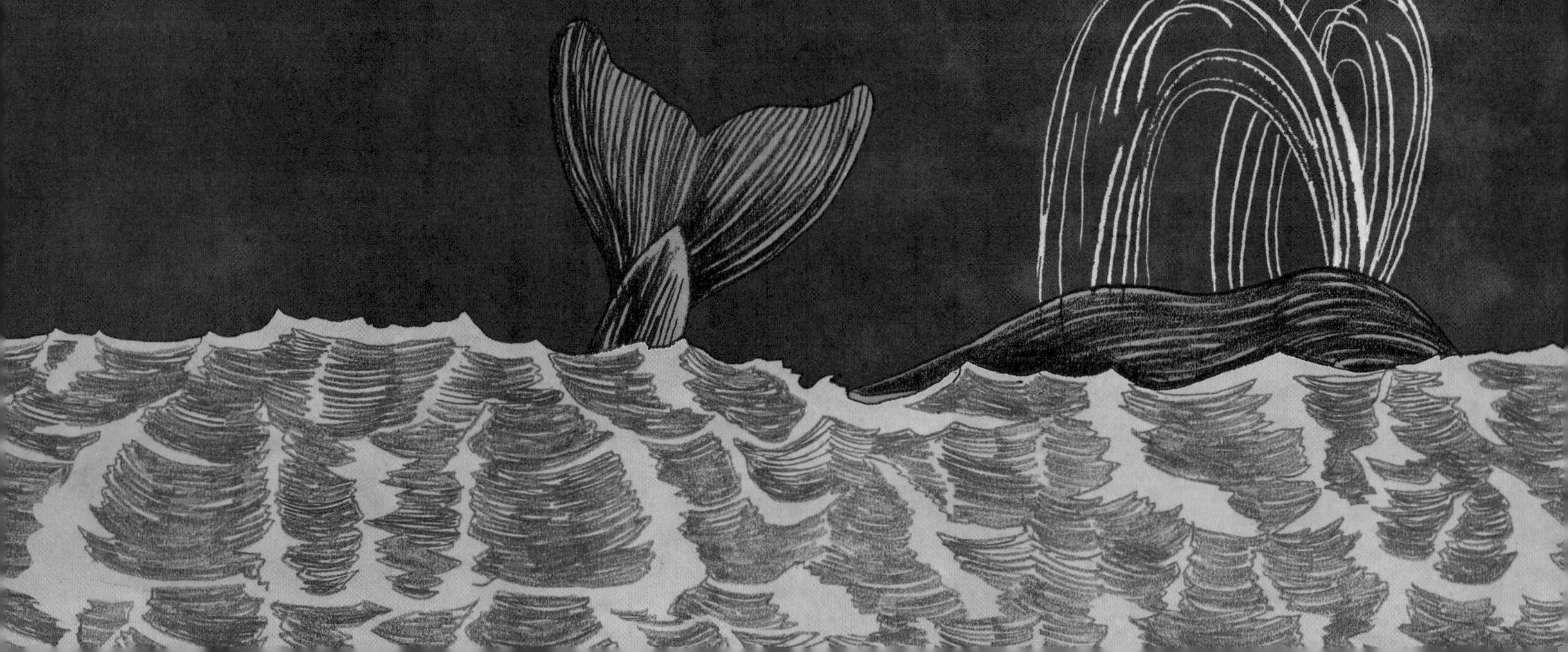

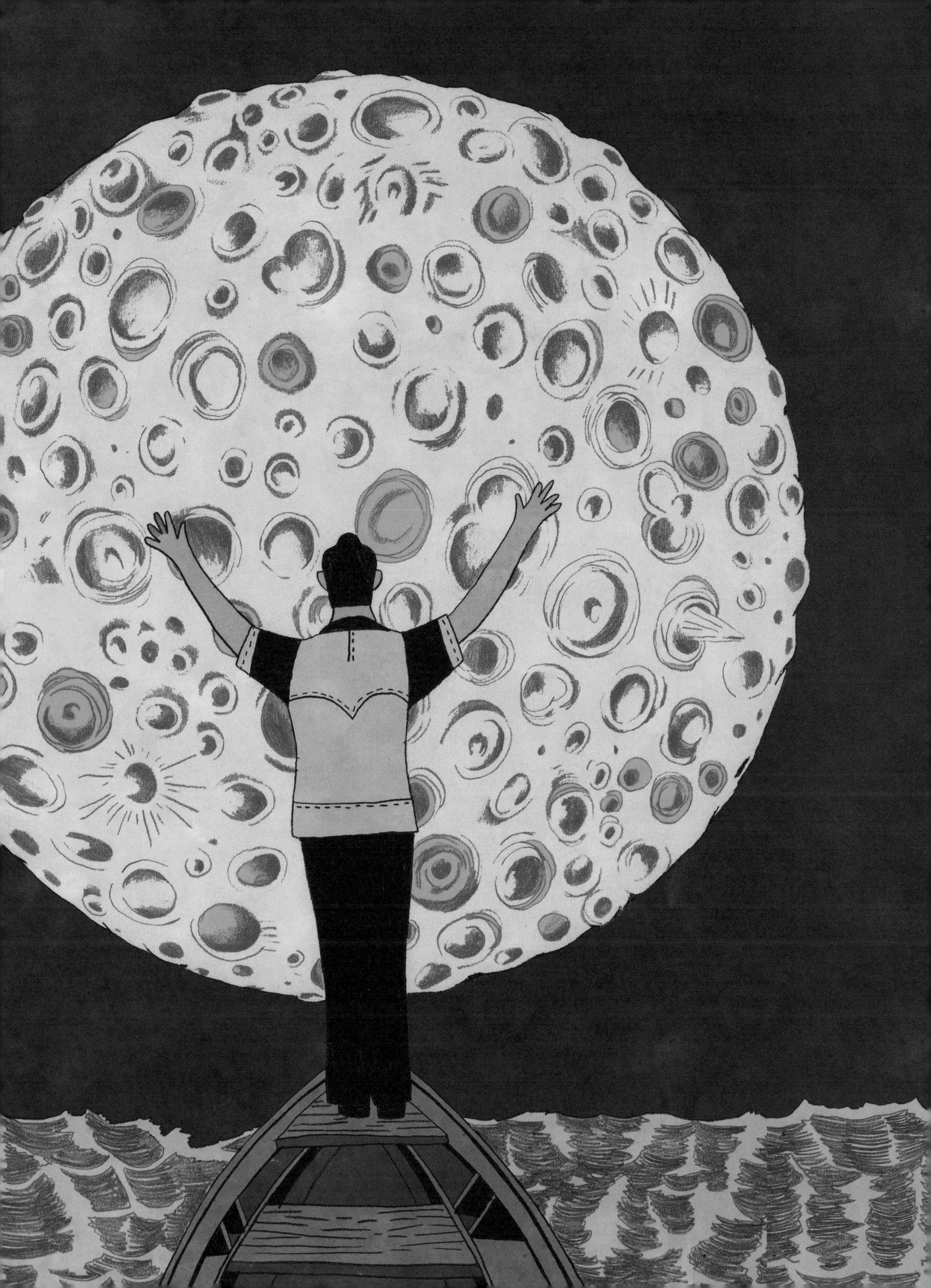

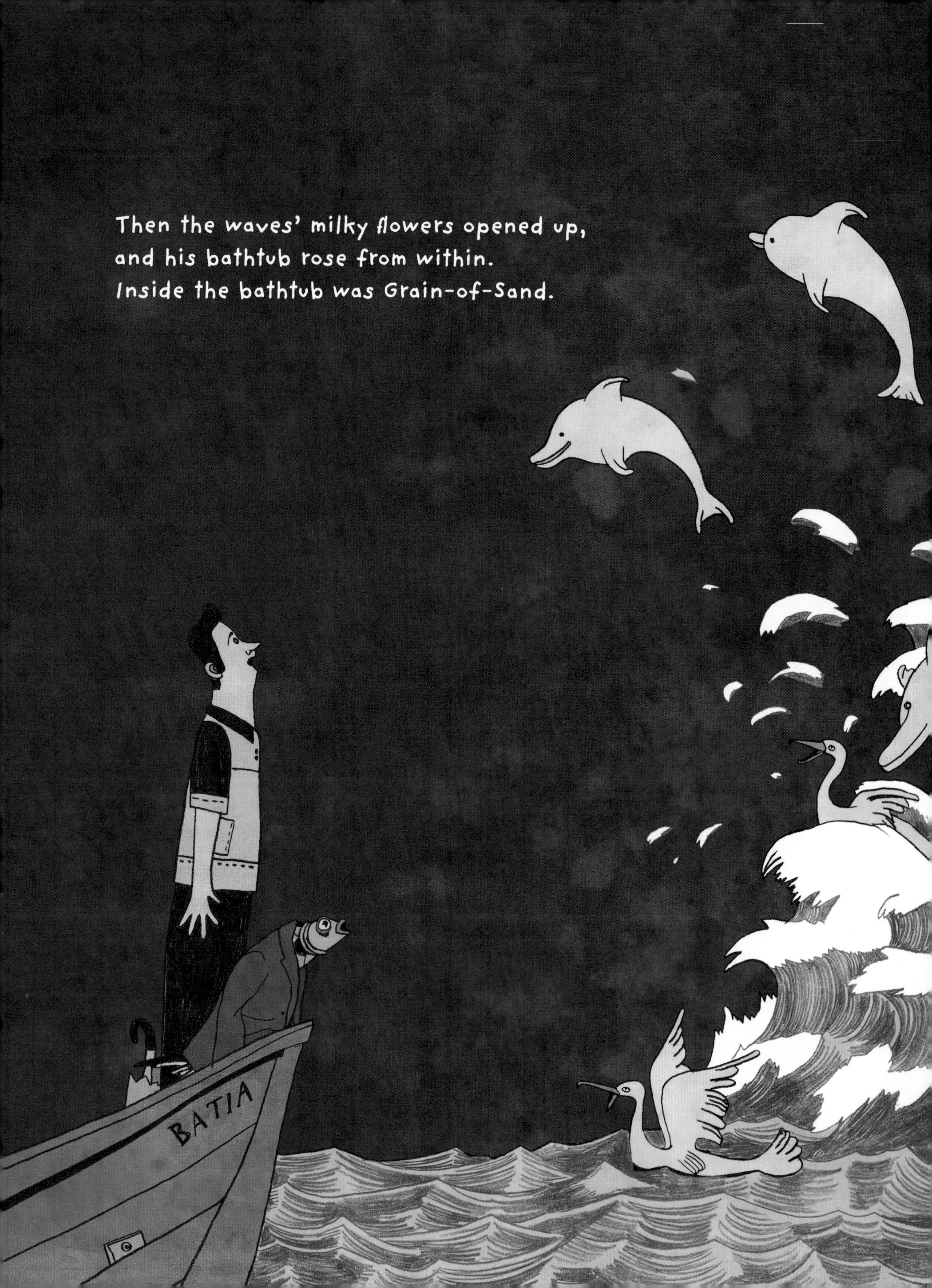
Then the waves' milky flowers opened up,
and his bathtub rose from within.
Inside the bathtub was Grain-of-Sand.
BATIA

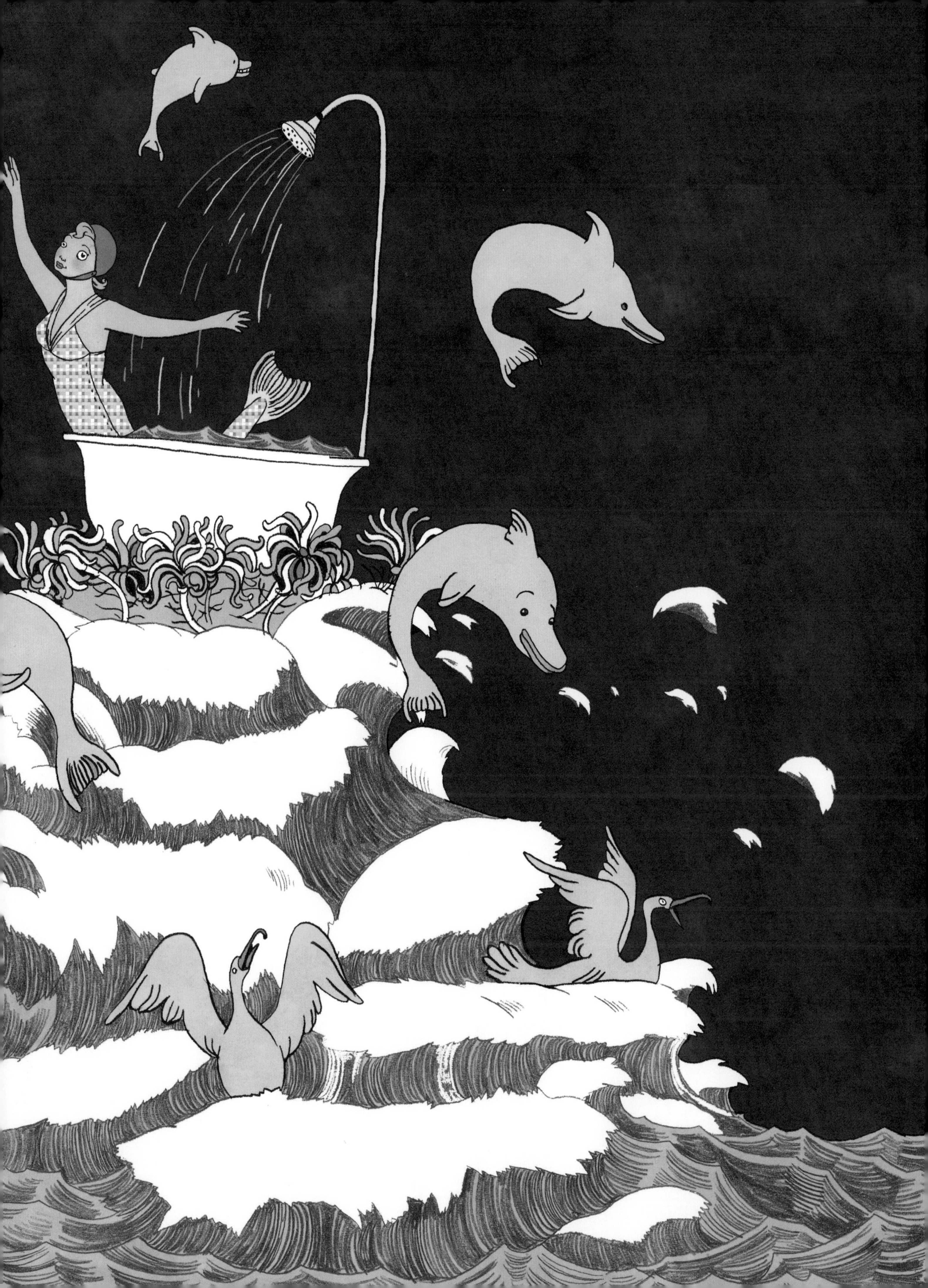

"Grain-of-Sand!" cried Mr. Whatwilltheysay,
and jumped from the boat straight into the bathtub.

"Good luck!" called the seagulls bobbing on the waves.

"Good luck!" cried the fishermen.

"Can you imagine what they'll say now?"
said Mr. Whatwilltheysay.

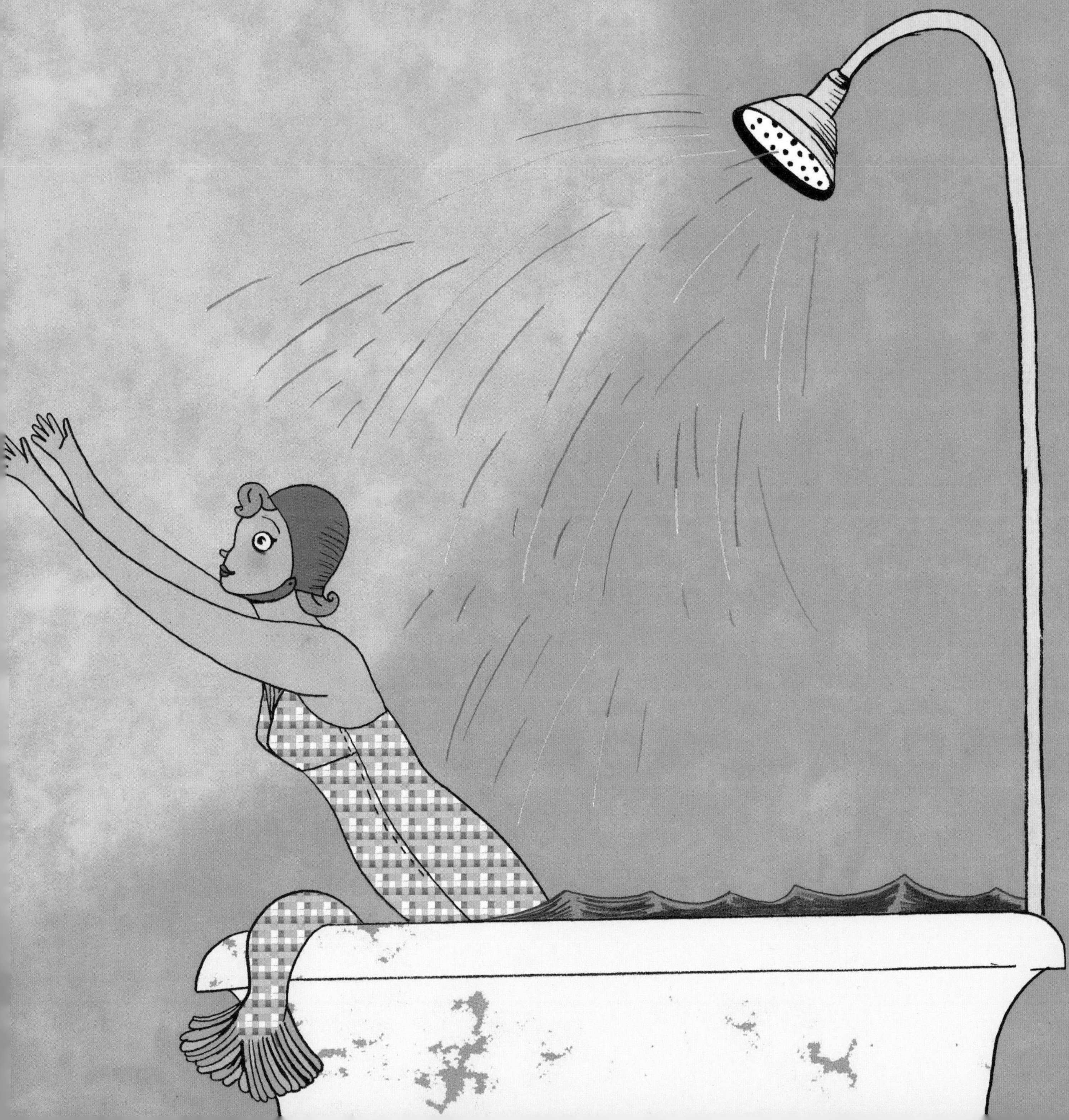

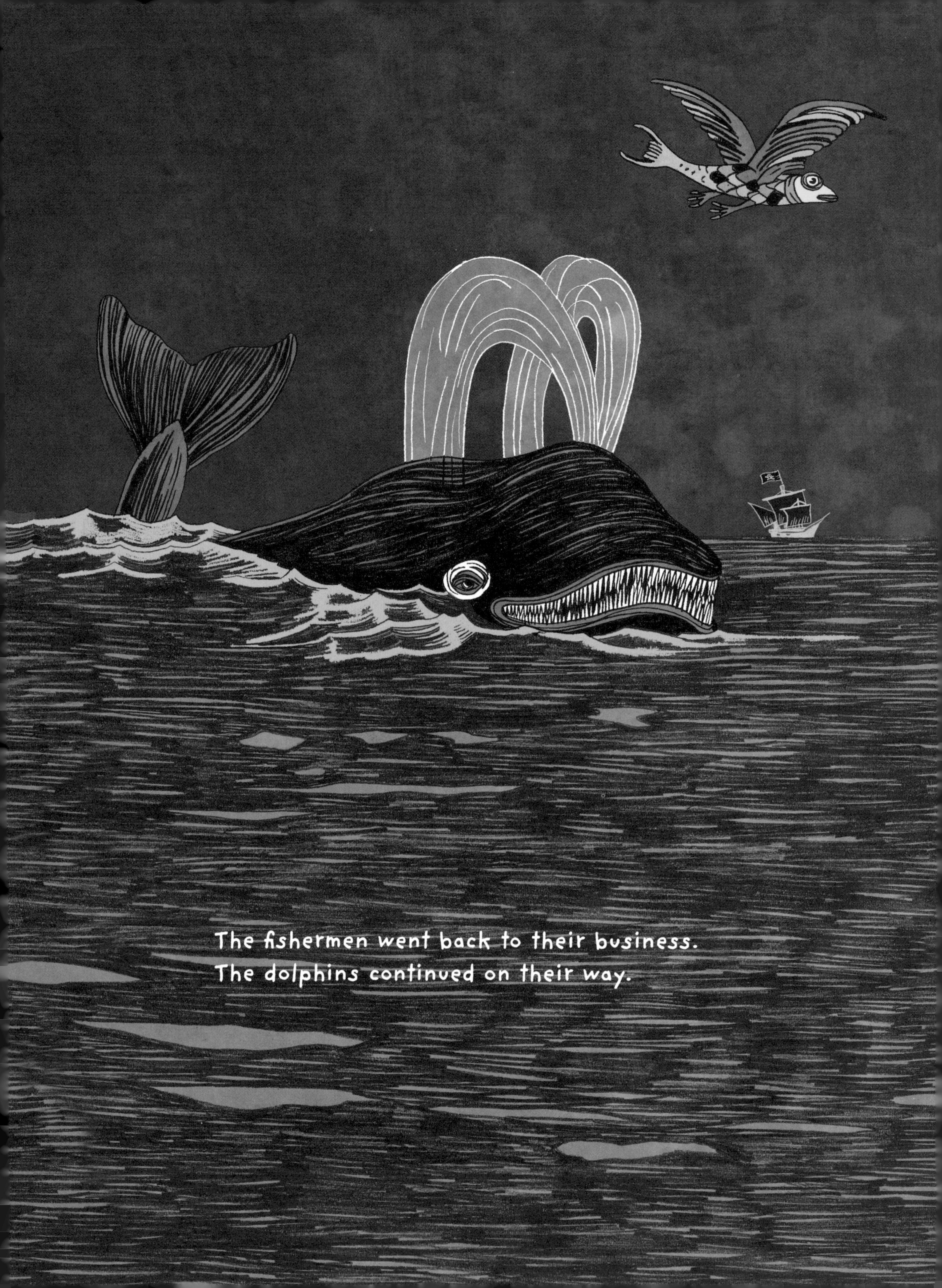

The fishermen went back to their business.
The dolphins continued on their way.

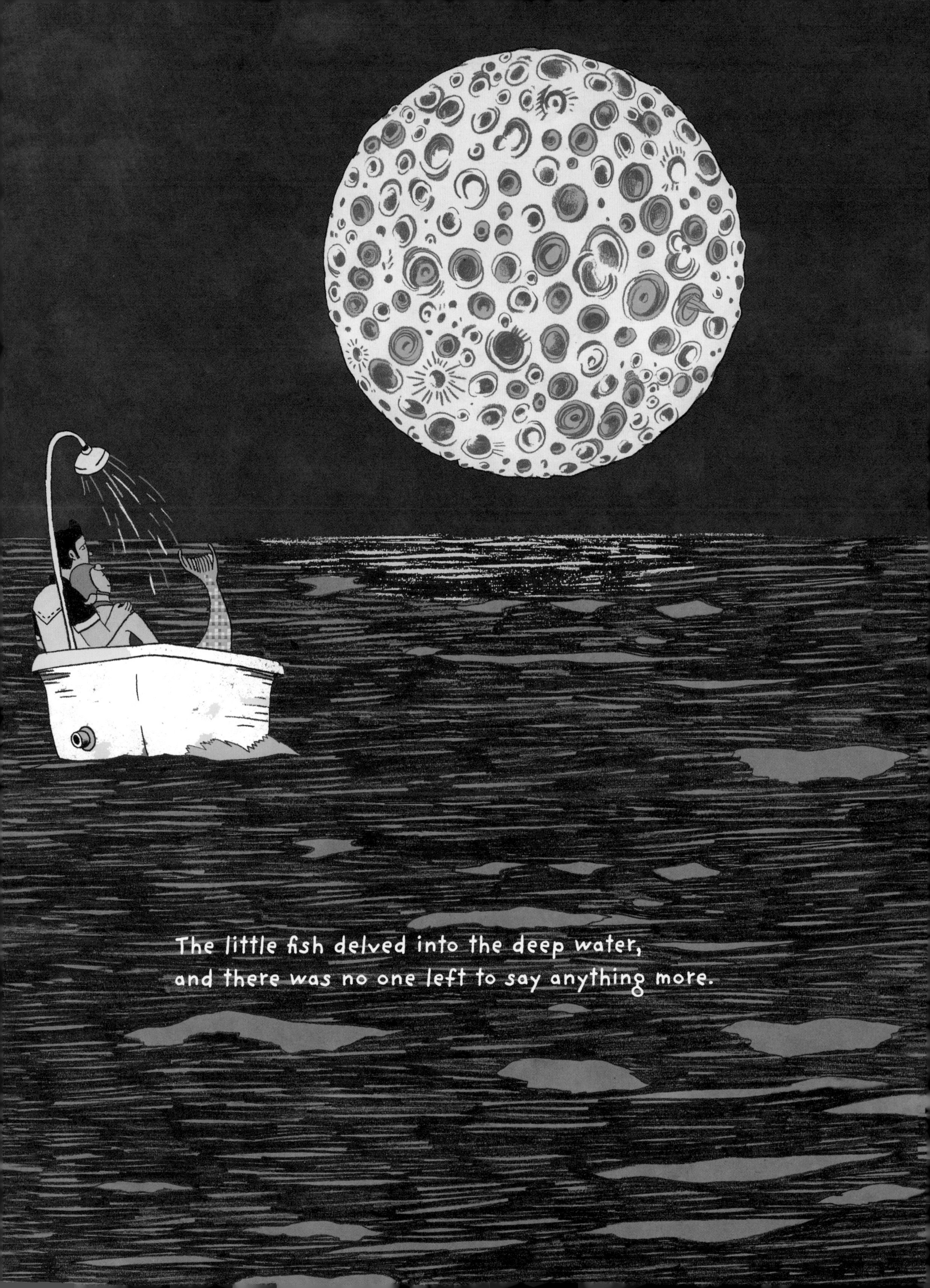
The little fish delved into the deep water,
and there was no one left to say anything more.

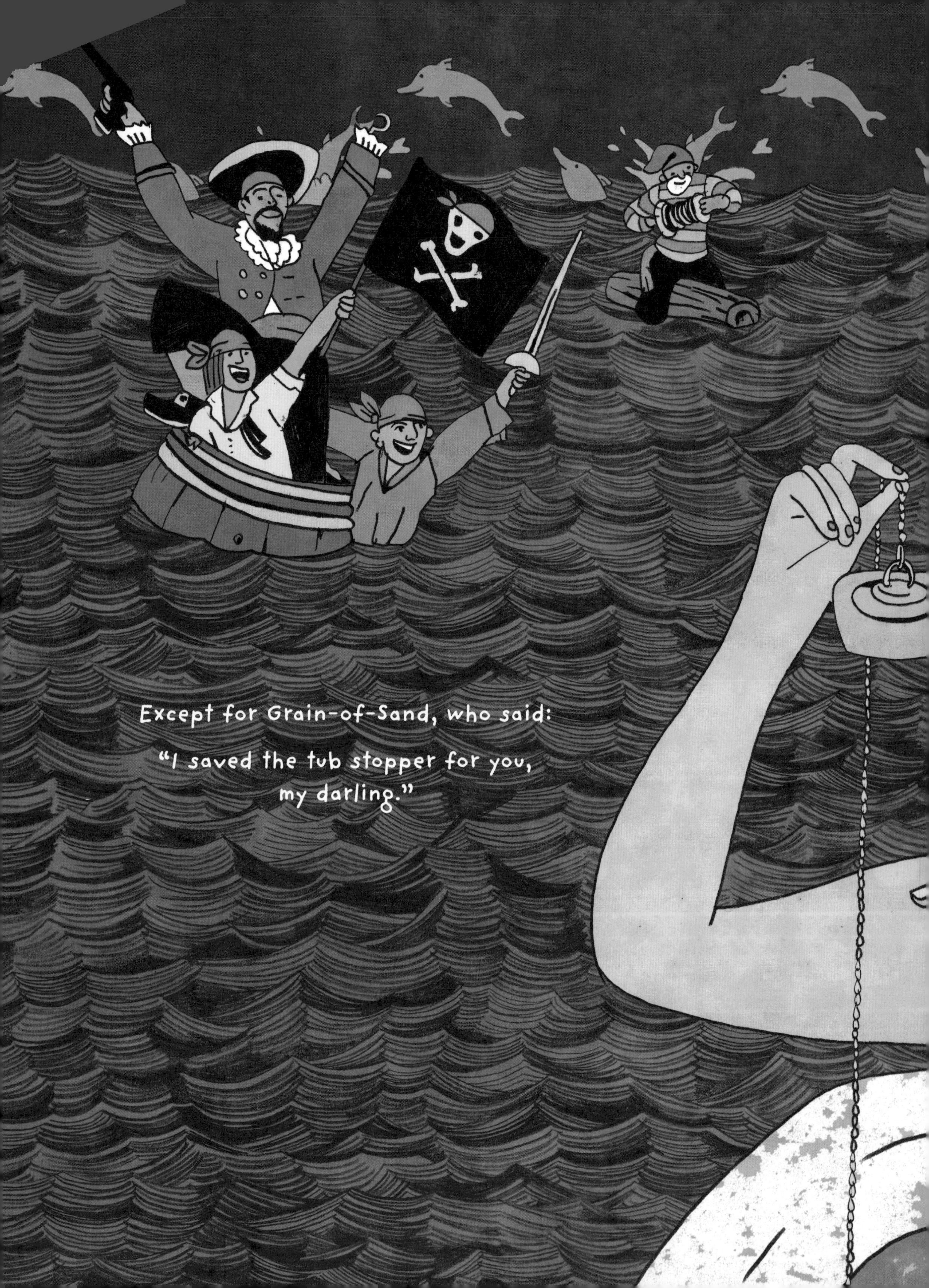

Except for Grain-of-Sand, who said:

"I saved the tub stopper for you, my darling."

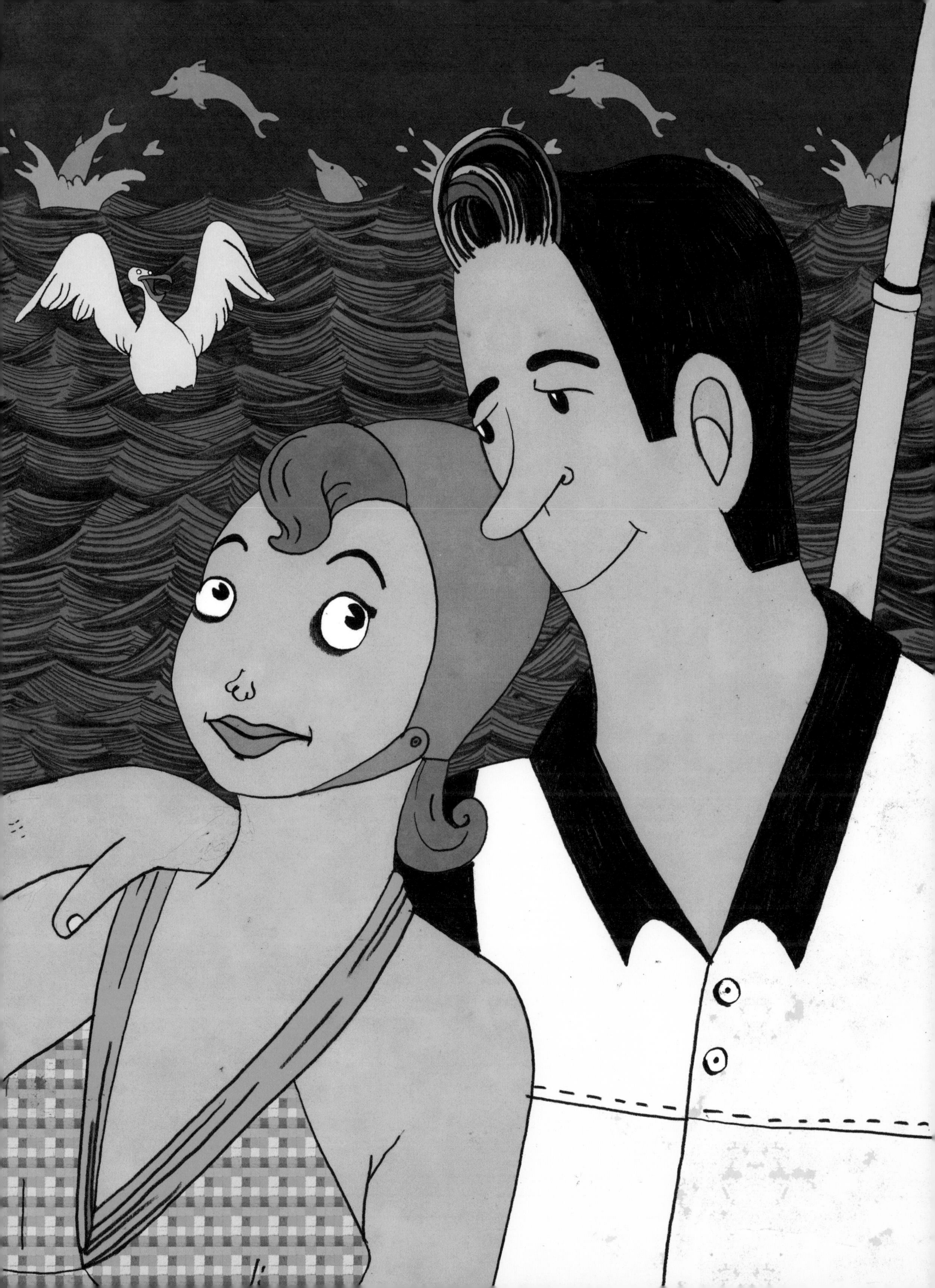

About the Author

Nurit Zarchi is an Israeli poet and author of books for adults and children. Zarchi has published many poems in children's magazines and more than one hundred works including children's books, poetry, prose, and research. Zarchi has received major Israeli awards, including the Bialik Prize and the Ze'ev Prize (four times), and she was twice the winner of the Prime Minister's Prize for her literary work.

About the Illustrator

Rutu Modan is an Israeli illustrator and comic book artist. She is a graduate of the Bezalel Academy of Arts and Design in Jerusalem and the former editor of the Hebrew edition of *MAD Magazine*. She received a Will Eisner Comic Industry Award for her book *Exit Wounds* in 2008.

About the Translator

Tal Goldfajn is an Assistant Professor of Hispanic Linguistics at the University of Massachusetts, Amherst. She holds a PhD in General Linguistics from the University of Oxford. She is the author of, among others books, *Word Order and Time in Biblical Hebrew Narrative* (Oxford University Press) and a co-editor of a special issue on *Translation and History in Latin America* published by the Estudios Interdisciplinarios de América Latina y el Caribe (Tel Aviv University). Her translations of plays by Nelson Rodrigues (from Brazilian Portuguese) and Sergi Belbel (from Spanish and Catalan) have been published by Asia Publishers and staged in Tel Aviv.

About Yonder

Yonder is an imprint from Restless Books devoted to bringing the wealth of great stories from around the globe to English-reading children, middle graders, and young adults. Books from other countries, cultures, viewpoints, and storytelling traditions can open up a universe of possibility, and the wider our view, the more powerfully books enrich and expand us. In an increasingly complex, globalized world, stories are potent vehicles of empathy. We believe it is essential to teach our kids to place themselves in the shoes of others beyond their communities, and instill in them a lifelong curiosity about the world and their place in it. Through publishing a diverse array of transporting stories, Yonder nurtures the next generation of savvy global citizens and lifelong readers.

Visit us at restlessbooks.org/yonder